When You're Young

SARAH WELK BAYNUM

Contents

Prologue

There are moments in this life that, even as they are happening, we know will be etched into our brains for the rest of our lives. Time may pass, life may change, and the events of our youth are drowned out by what adulthood brings.

But still, there are memories that even time and age can't touch because they have become a part of who we are. For Emma Walker, that memory is of this very day.

Thirteen-year-old Emma didn't expect today to be different than any other day at the barn. Grabbing the bag of carrots out of her backpack that she brought from home, Emma walked into the barn and headed straight for Razz's stall, the horse she was leasing. Breathing in the sweet smell of horses and hay, Emma rounded the corner towards the row of stalls where the gelding was stabled.

But what she saw when she approached his stall made her heart sink. Maggie, her riding instructor, the barn owner, Mr. Cromwell, and two people she didn't recognize were huddled around Razz's stall.

"Is something wrong with him?" she had thought, her heart starting to race.

Maggie turned around when she heard footfalls on the barn aisle. "Oh, Emma," Maggie said, her voice low and breathy as her concerned gaze met Emma's.

"What's wrong?" Emma asked quickly, her eyes darting from Maggie back to Razz's stall.

Maggie said nothing but walked over to Emma and wrapped an arm around her shoulders, gently leading her outside.

"Maggie...," Emma's voice broke after she said her trainer's name. Emma knew Maggie well enough to know whatever was going on was very, very bad.

Maggie sat on the bench next to the outdoor arena and Emma followed suit. "Emma, do you remember when you first started leasing Razz, how I said it was going to be on a month-to-month basis?" Maggie asked. Emma nodded, feeling a tightness in her throat.

"Well, we had to do it that way because Razz's owner owed the barn owner a lot of money in back board, and we had not heard from her in several months. We weren't sure if his owner would ever come back, or if he had been essentially abandoned here, but I know how much you loved riding him so we agreed to allow a lease under those conditions. Does that make sense?" Maggie asked.

Emma only nodded again, knowing she was on the verge of tears, and if she spoke, that would be it.

Maggie sighed and took Emma's hand, placing hers over Emma's. "Honey, Razz's owner is here and just paid off his back board. She is taking him to another barn...right now," Maggie said.

The reality of what Maggie was saying hit Emma like a ton of bricks. Razz was leaving, and he was never coming back.

Tears spilled silently down Emma's cheeks. "Can I say goodbye?" Emma asked, barely croaking out the words.

"I'll clear everyone out and give you a few minutes with him," Maggie said, squeezing her hand and giving her a sad smile.

Emma walked back into the barn with Maggie who asked the owner to step outside for a moment with her. Pressing her forehead to Razz's forelock, Emma felt tears dripping onto his soft fur. She pulled away, looking him over as she ran her hand down his neck. "I'll never forget you," she murmured to the gelding, who playfully nosed her in the chest. She smiled a little through her tears.

"I'm sorry Emma," Maggie's voice said from down the aisle. Emma looked up and saw Razz's owner walking quickly down the aisle with a lead rope in her hand.

Emma stepped aside, wiping tears away as she watched him being led out of the barn towards the waiting horse trailer. Emma jogged out of barn and watched them load Razz in the trailer, knowing that was the last she would see of the first horse she ever loved. It wasn't until the trailer was halfway down the road and completely out of sight that Emma walked slowly back into the barn.

Sliding down a stall door, she sat there in the dirt aisle on the ground. Maggie was standing in the entrance of the barn looking over at her with a strange expression. "I'll be right back!" Maggie said, sounding suspiciously excited.

"Great, she is probably going to go find some other horse for me to ride today," Emma thought. It wasn't that Emma wasn't grateful to ride any horse she had the opportunity to ride, but today, she just wanted to miss the horse she'd lost. Maybe Maggie thought finding another horse to ride for the day would cheer her up, but Emma knew it would only make her miss Razz that much more.

Emma wasn't sure how long Maggie had been gone. Twenty minutes, maybe? What was she doing? Tacking up the horse for her? Maggie peeked only her head around the aisle of the barn Emma was still in.

"Emma, stand up but do not turn around, and close your eyes!" Maggie said.

Emma kept her eyes shut but spun around anyway to face the direction Maggie's voice came from.

"Why are my eyes closed?" Emma asked.

"Because I have a surprise for you. Now, before you open your eyes, there's something I want you to know first. You will have to work really hard, but the barn owners have agreed to let you feed horses, turn out, and clean stalls on weekends...and in exchange...,"

Emma's eyes flew open before Maggie was finished with her speech. She gasped audibly and stared wide-eyed at the seventeen hand, dark bay Thoroughbred gelding in front of her. She recognized him; he had arrived at the barn as a sale horse but was a little older, so she remembered Maggie saying they were being extra picky about buyers because of his age. They wanted to find him the right home, and it dawned on her in that moment that the right home just might be her.

"Wait, are you saying he's *mine*? No way, my parents can't afford a horse...," Emma began.

"Well, Miss Emma, if you had let me finish!" Maggie said, scolding young Emma with a laugh. "Yes, he is yours, and yes, I called your parents and they are able to pay the difference. As I was saying, you will have to be here *every* weekend to care for *your* horse and the other horses at the barn too, but that will significantly reduce the board costs. Of course, you can still help me out in exchange for weekly lessons like you have been doing."

Still wide-eyed, Emma approached her first horse slowly, almost in awe. "Hi Lexington," she whispered to him.

Taking his lead rope from Maggie, knowing he was hers, that was all the motivation she needed.

Chapter One

JUNIOR YEAR OF HIGH SCHOOL, 2006

Sixteen-year-old Emma caught herself falling asleep for the second time this class.

"Horse show hangovers are awful, but totally worth it," she thought, sitting straighter in her chair and forcing her eyes to stay open as her math teacher continued to describe the equation on the board.

Math was already not her strong suit, so between the lack of sleep and the physical exhaustion she felt, there was no way she was going to retain the information the teacher had just gone over.

"Alright class, grab a partner and try this worksheet to see how you do working the problems out on your own," the teacher said, passing a piece of paper to each student.

"I assume we are going to be partners as usual?" Melissa said to Emma when they received their worksheets.

"Always," Emma said smiling, sliding her chair closer to her friend.

The thing she liked best about being in math class with Melissa was that her friend despised math almost as much as she did. That, however, was their downfall when it came to partnering up on worksheets.

"Question one," Melissa began aloud, "What is the slope?"

Both girls stared blankly at each other a moment before Emma answered, "Yes?"

Melissa laughed, writing "yes" next to the question.

"Ok, so we know there is a slope, but we don't know what it is. We'll just circle back to that one," Melissa said rolling her eyes. The girls struggled through the remaining six questions shortly before they heard the teacher's voice at the front of the classroom.

"Time's up! Let's go over the answers quickly. Did anyone get the first answer right?"

Several hands shot up, neither of which were Emma's nor Melissa's. The bell rang exactly eleven minutes later, and Emma couldn't grab her backpack and leave her last class of the day fast enough.

"Our torture session for the day is officially complete," Melissa said, blowing out a breath the as girls walked out of the classroom together. "By the way, how did your horse show go yesterday?"

"Great, actually! Lexington and I got second in our division. He was a good boy, as usual. I am paying for it today though; we didn't get home until almost midnight since the show was out of town."

"That's great! It makes sense why you all but fell out of your chair falling asleep in class today, though," Melissa said, elbowing Emma in the side playfully.

"So, it was that obvious, huh?" Emma replied, letting out an audible sigh as she tucked a piece of her light brown hair behind her ear.

"Just a little," Melissa said, grinning broadly.

The girls headed to their respective lockers, which were only about five lockers apart, and swapped books from their backpacks.

"How was your last class of the day?" Kaylin, one of their mutual friends, asked Melissa and Emma as she rounded the corner from where her locker was located.

"Pretty much as exciting as math can be," Emma said, slamming her locker shut and rolling her eyes.

"I take it you're still horse show hungover?" Kaylin said with a laugh, knowing the feeling all too well herself. Emma was glad for a friends like Kaylin at school who got the whole "horse crazy" thing, even if she did ride at a different barn.

Melissa was supportive of the whole horse thing and was always asking how her horse was or how Kaylin's lessons went. Still, she would never truly understand the mind of a horse crazy teenager like a fellow horse lover would.

"Definitely horse show hungover," Emma replied, laughing. "Do you still have your riding lesson on Wednesday? I'll come watch if you want!"

"Yes, you should come! Now that I'm officially a licensed Ohio driver, you can just catch a ride with me," Kaylin said, proudly pulling out her freshly minted driver's license for her friends to see. The girls gushed over the shiny plastic and started talking about how much longer it would be until they started driving too.

"I have my driving test scheduled for next week; I'm so excited," Emma added, beaming. Having the freedom to drive herself to the barn was something she had dreamed about for years. Not that her parents weren't great about taking her to the barn on weekends when she worked there, or a few days during the week when she had a lesson or wanted to hack her horse. But knowing she could hop into a car and drive there on her own felt very grown up and exciting.

The girls chatted all the way to the bus stop, only stopping when they were forced to say goodbye as each of them climbed into their respective buses. Emma watched jealously from the bus window as Kaylin turned toward the parking lot and her parents' car that she had driven to school.

"Only six more days and that could be me," she thought. Images of driving down the country roads toward the barn filled her mind as she stared out the foggy bus window.

ell

While she had promised her horse and her trainer she wouldn't ride the day after the show, Emma still had begged her mom to take her to the barn that afternoon after school anyway.

"I'll be over here reading my book if you need me, hon," Chrissy, Emma's mother, said as she walked to the shaded area near the arena that had a wooden bench.

Emma knew her horse deserved a good grooming and a liniment treatment on his legs. At least, that was her excuse for needing to come out today.

Truthfully, Emma knew she could spend every single day at the barn. The spring air was crisp, but warm, making a long, cold winter of indoor riding in the small indoor arena seem like a distant memory now.

Spring weather in Ohio had only showed its face a few weeks ago, and ever since, Emma couldn't get enough of being outside and in the barn. The sunshine had made today's high temperature a perfect sixty-eight degrees, so even though her horse needed a day off, the thought of grooming and hand grazing him still appealed to her.

Emma walked towards the tack room to grab her grooming box and liniment as she enjoyed the warm air and horse smells around her.

"Hey, Lex," she cooed to the gelding as she slid the halter over his head, leading him from the stall. Clipping him to the cross-ties, she took a moment to scratch his withers in his favorite place, giggling when his upper lip twitched in response. The gelding was nothing short of a character.

Emma curried the dust off her horse which landed on her despite her attempts to lean away from the grime flying off his fur.

"Dust transfer season," she murmured to herself, smiling even though she was getting filthy.

Sometimes Emma couldn't believe she was lucky enough to own her own horse, even three years later. After all, she had been a horse crazy kid since the age of nine. Emma still remembered doing anything and everything to just be *near* a horse. Years ago, before she started taking lessons with Maggie, she had volunteered at a non-profit for just the chance to groom and be near horses.

Laughter echoed from the other end of the "L" shaped barn, pulling Emma from her thoughts.

Emma rolled her eyes, recognizing who the voice and the laughter belonged to: Luke Cromwell. All the girls at school talked about how cute they thought Luke was, going on and on about his jaw line. Emma wasn't sure what all the fuss was about; he looked like any other teenage boy at school to her.

"Great," Emma mumbled to herself, beginning to brush her horse with a little extra flip of her wrist now.

Another boy's voice could be heard faintly too, then another.

"How many friends does he need to have over at the same time?" she thought.

Was one friend not sufficient enough? Was it really necessary to invite your *entire* entourage over? And more importantly, was it necessary to bring them into the barn where they had no business being? After all, Luke didn't ride horses. At least, not anymore.

"What a waste," Emma thought, half stomping to the tack room to grab a bottle of the waterless-bath spray she left in her tack trunk. It didn't make any sense to her why the son of the barn owner didn't ride. If her family owned an entire boarding barn...

She stopped herself from dwelling on such a fantasy. That would never be her life. She had Lexington, lessons with Maggie, and her friends. That was all she needed to be happy. At least, that was the logic she was using to keep herself from being jealous of Luke Cromwell.

The boys' voices grew louder, and Emma braced herself, knowing they were seconds from rounding the corner to the part of the barn she was in. Why are teenage boys *so* loud all the time?

"Oh, hey Emma. I didn't know you were here," Luke said, and his group of buddies chuckled in the background. They clearly had no interest in being around horses, and it rubbed her the wrong way every time. Why couldn't they go run around in one of the unused back pastures and talk about whatever sport they had been yelling about a few moments ago?

"You're going to scare my horse," Emma said, first looking at Luke, then the boys behind him. Her expression hardened in detest.

"Sorry," Luke said. Emma couldn't tell if he meant it or not. His tone implied he might *actually* be sorry. His buddies chuckled louder in the background again, making an "oh" sound, dramatizing her words. Luke turned around, joining his friends in their laughter. Any passing thought of his sincerity vanished after that.

Emma turned around, face flushed pink. She decided to ignore them and hoped they would simply go away when they realized she wasn't interested in their drama.

Emma clipped the lead rope to Lexington's halter and unclipped him from the cross-ties. She began leading her horse forward, directly into the path of the three boys.

"This should get them moving," she thought smugly.

"Hey! Your stupid horse is going to run us over!" one of the boys said, leaping out of the way.

Emma turned towards the boy, a look of fury on her face. "Don't talk about my horse that way," she said with a venomous tone.

The boy's eyes widened at her words, but then he laughed again. Emma had half a mind to *actually* run him over with her horse.

She kept walking out of the barn doors, not looking back at the boys still chuckling behind her. Emma didn't stop until the boys' laughter was completely out of earshot.

Boys were infuriating. Why did her friends seem so crazy over them? Horses were so much better than boys. They never judged, they loved unconditionally, and they were perfect in every way, in her opinion.

"You're the only boy I need," Emma whispered to Lexington, her chin resting on the bridge of his nose. She let her horse have his head back, and he began pulling up thick mouthfuls of bright green grass.

Emma leaned against his barrel, staring out at the endless pastures around her. She took a deep breath, letting it out slowly as she tried to clear her mind of the annoying teenage boys still lurking somewhere in the barn.

Emma shut her locker door and picked her backpack up off the floor.

Kaylin and Melissa were waiting for her at the end of the row of lockers. They always walked to first period class together since it was the only class all three of them shared this year. It had become a bit of a morning ritual for them.

"How was everyone's evening yesterday?" Melissa asked in a cheerful voice. Emma tossed her friend a warm smile, deciding not to go into her run in with Luke Cromwell quite so early in the morning.

"I watched *Miss Congeniality* last night," Kaylin said with a smile.

Melissa laughed, shooting Kaylin a look. "For the hundredth time?"

"It was on TV," Kaylin replied with a shrug.

"It is a good movie. I mean I've lost track of how many times I've seen it too," Emma added in Kaylin's defense.

"Thank you! I'm glad someone else appreciates it as much as I do," Kaylin replied, shooting Melissa a smug look.

"I'm not saying it's *not* a good movie, just that I don't think I could watch it as many times as the two of you have," Melissa teased.

The three friends began crossing the part of the hallway that intersected with where the freshman lockers were located. As they stepped into the middle of the hallway, the bell rang, signaling to anyone still in the hall that classes were beginning.

None of the girls changed their pace and kept walking casually towards their first class of the day only a few more classrooms down.

Suddenly, a freshman with one of the backpacks that rolled behind her, like a suitcase, came sprinting down the freshman hallway. Melissa and Kaylin turned their heads in the half a second before the freshman was practically on top of them.

Emma, however, did not notice the oncoming freshman.

The freshman, and her backpack, ran right into Emma's legs. Not expecting the impact, Emma lost her balance and faceplanted onto the backpack that had taken her out. She laid there on top of the backpack, wondering what hit her.

The freshman's eyes went wide, and then the skin between her eyes bunched in distain. The freshman grabbed the handle of the backpack and began ruthlessly yanking it from Emma's lifeless-looking body without mercy.

Emma rolled, getting off the backpack before it was yanked completely out from under her. The freshman frantically began running towards her classroom, backpack in tow, without a second glance.

Emma rolled her eyes. "Freshman," she muttered, picking herself up off the ground.

"Someone needs to give that girl a chill pill," Melissa said, crossing her arms across her chest as she watched the student still sprinting down the hallway.

"I thought horse girls had good balance," a male voice said from somewhere behind her.

Emma and her friends turned around simultaneously, scowling in the direction of the male voice.

"Excuse me?!" Emma said as she turned around. Emma's cheeks flushed pink and her stomach sank.

There stood Luke Cromwell and his entourage of annoying friends, feet away from them. They had clearly seen everything, and Luke's friend Chad had decided to make her day worse with his commentary.

"Being trampled by a freshman has nothing to do with good balance," Kaylin said in Emma's defense.

"Can't you find someone else to annoy?" Emma said, her tone giving away her detest for Luke and his friends.

"Aren't you boys late for class anyway?" Melissa added.

"*That* was worth being late for class for," another of Luke's friends chided.

Emma's eyes locked with Luke. He flashed her a grin prompting Emma to roll her eyes again. What was he smiling about? Who smiles at someone faceplanting? Did that boy have no manners?

"Let's go," Emma said, still glaring at Luke.

All three girls turned around and powerwalked towards their classroom. The sound of the boys laughing could still be heard behind them as they walked.

"I didn't know you knew Luke Cromwell," Melissa whispered, so only Emma and Kaylin could hear. Until that moment, they had never spoken a single word to each other at school.

"I don't. I mean, not really. His dad owns the barn where I board Lexington," Emma replied.

"Seriously? That's unfortunate," Kaylin replied, shaking her head.

"You have no idea," Emma replied.

"Want my new boyfriend to give him a talking to or something?" Melissa said, a smitten look on her face. Melissa had been blissfully dating a boy named Johnny for exactly two weeks.

"That's ok, I can handle Luke and his posse. Thanks anyway though," Emma said to Melissa. The last thing Emma needed was her best friend's boyfriend defending her. She had a feeling that would only make things worse.

Melissa smiled sympathetically at Emma. "Ok, well, if you change your mind, let me know."

Emma was glad when the conversation shifted to a play-by-play of how Melissa's new relationship was going. Even if it was a little nauseating to hear her go on and on about Johnny, she was glad to get her mind off those infuriating boys.

"Good luck, honey!" Emma's mother said loudly as she waved from the sidewalk of the BMV.

"Thanks!" Emma said, not quite as loudly.

The day had finally come: the day she took her driver's test.

Daydreams of driving down the open road towards the barn on her own had been clouding her mind and distracting her from schoolwork all week long.

Emma climbed into the passenger side of her parents' mini-van, and the BMV employee who would be testing her slid into the passenger seat.

"Ok," he looked down at his clipboard, seeming to forget who he was testing. "Emma, my name is Ernest. We are going to head out of the parking lot and make a right onto that road," he said, using his pen to point out the direction they would be taking.

"Got it," Emma said. The death grip she had on the steering wheel was turning her knuckles white. Ernest's eyes flitted to her steering wheel death grip, then to her determined expression.

"Just relax, I'm sure you'll do fine," he said.

Emma bit her lip but relaxed her grip on the steering wheel. Clearly Ernest didn't realize just how important passing her driving test was.

Emma put her foot on the gas, but just a little too hard. The minivan jumped forward and Ernest gasped audibly.

"Oops. Sorry," Emma said sheepishly, tossing the driving instructor an apologetic look. Her nerves were getting the best of her. She reminded herself to relax before Ernest flunked her before she even left the parking lot. Ernest motioned back to the road, then scribbled something down on his paperwork.

Emma pressed on the gas pedal again, gentler this time, and turned onto the side street. She glanced down at the speedometer every few seconds, worried she might accidentally be going too fast. Ernest instructed her to turn left onto the next road. Emma stopped at the stop sign, counting to ten in her mind. No way she was losing points on a rolling stop.

By the time they had circled back to the parking lot of the BMV, Emma was feeling confident in her driving abilities.

"I think I'm passing!" she thought.

"Up ahead are the cones where you will be performing the parallel parking portion of the test. Please pull through and then back through the cones," Ernest instructed.

Emma swallowed hard. This was the most challenging part of the test.

She slowly crept the minivan up to the entrance of the arranged cones. Emma used her side mirrors to make sure the back end of the van wouldn't clip the cones as she pulled through. She stopped at the end, waiting for Ernest's signal. He was scratching notes on his paperwork again.

"Go ahead and back through," he said.

Emma looked at the cones in her rearview mirror. It was hard to tell where the cones began curving in this minivan. She began backing up slowly, checking her mirrors every couple seconds.

"I can't see anything in this van!" she thought. It was that exact moment she felt the tire of the van clip an invisible cone on her right.

"Sorry, that's an automatic failure," Ernest said, pressing his lips together and frantically writing on his paperwork.

Emma put her head on the steering wheel and let out a sigh. Just like that, all her dreams of driving herself to the barn were up in smoke.

"I'll pick you up at 6:00 pm!" Emma's mother said as she dropped her off at the barn.

Emma waved, then sighed audibly.

"I should be driving myself to the barn right now," she thought.

She would if she hadn't failed her driver's test, that is. Emma decided not to let her poor mood over her failed driver's test ruin a perfectly nice day at the barn. Lexington hung his head over the stall guard, letting out a low nicker when he saw Emma.

Emma felt the gloom hanging over her head lift away as his big brown eyes connected with hers. Her hand met his soft coat as it ran down his neck. Horses had a special way of making her feel better, even on her worst day.

"How is my good boy today?" she asked, pulling a mint from her pocket. The crinkling sound had Lexington's ears zeroing in on the treat in her hand. He snatched it up and crunched it slowly.

"I thought you were taking your driver's test today," a voice said behind her, making her jump.

Emma turned around to see Luke leaning against the wooden barn wall, his arms crossed over his chest. Emma scanned his expression, looking for the meaning behind his words.

"How did you even know my driver's test was today?" Emma replied, defense leaking into her tone.

"I overheard you and Maggie talking last week," Luke said with a shrug. He casually ran his fingers through his dirty blonde hair.

Emma's eyes narrowed. "So, you were eavesdropping then."

"I wasn't exactly eavesdropping," Luke replied, raising an eyebrow.

Emma shot him a look of annoyance. She wasn't sure how to refute that. "Why are you always hanging around the barn anyway? You don't even ride!"

"Last time I checked, this was *my* dad's barn," Luke replied.

Emma's jaw stiffened. She hated that he had a point. Still, why did he feel the need to roam around when he had no interest in horses? As much as she despised Luke, she didn't want to say anything that would cause problems for her with his father, Mr. Cromwell. After all, his father was the reason she had a horse in the first place. Without Mr. Cromwell allowing her to work off most of her horse's board, her parents would never have been able to afford a horse. That, and she didn't want to cause issues for Maggie, who worked as Mr. Cromwell's trainer.

"You're right Luke, this *is* your barn," Emma snapped back, trying to keep most of the venom out of her words.

Luke seemed amused by this. She hated letting him win this argument, but it wasn't worth risking her or Maggie's jobs.

"Did your friends get sick of you or something?" Emma added. She was glad his slew of friends weren't here for once. Still, Luke by himself was plenty annoying. Why did he drive her *so* crazy?

"They are all at practice," he said shrugging.

Shoot. That was a good excuse. Not that she planned to admit that to Luke.

"Why don't you play sports too?" Emma asked, although she wasn't sure why. It's not like she cared, but it seemed odd that all of his friends played sports and he didn't. They all seemed attached at the hip any other time.

Luke shifted his weight looking uncomfortable. Emma resisted urge to smirk at his discomfort.

He shrugged again. "I'm just not that into them."

"You used to ride though, right? That is a sport you know," Emma said. She was ready to correct Luke the second he tried to tell her it wasn't a sport. It wasn't the first time someone had tried to tell her riding wasn't a sport. Emma now had an endless list of facts in her mind waiting to help her win that argument, just in case.

"Yeah, I did," Luke said, his gaze dropping to the ground. He kicked at a small pile of dirt in front of him.

Emma was surprised by his reaction. Surprised, and a little disappointed she couldn't use her slew of facts about horses being a sport on Luke.

"Why don't you ride anymore?" Emma pressed. She was curious now. She had been for a while, actually.

His gaze snapped from the ground to meet Emma's. He had a strange look on his face, but it quickly vanished and he cleared his throat.

"That's not really any of your business," he said. Emma heard something strange in his tone. Sadness maybe? It didn't really make any sense. Emma wanted to push for answers but reminded herself ticking Luke off too much could have repercussions.

"Whatever," Emma said, turning her attention back on her horse and away from Luke.

She didn't turn back around until she heard Luke's footfalls leave the barn.

Emma pulled Lexington out and started to tack him up, but for some reason, she was still wondering why Luke had acted strangely when she had asked about him not riding anymore.

Emma walked towards the locker room with one strap of her gym bag slung over her shoulder. She pushed open the door and accidentally whacked one of her classmates, Jaclyn Alcott, in the face.

"Oh gee, I'm sorry Jac," Emma said, inadvertently using the nickname she had for her former friend.

"Watch where you are going, Emma," Jaclyn said viciously.

"Sorry," Emma mumbled, her eyes dropping to the ground. Of all the people she could have taken out with a door it *had* to be Jaclyn. It seemed odd they had been close friends once. If Jaclyn passed her in the hallway now, she didn't even acknowledge Emma existed. It had been hard for Emma to accept that she and

Jac were no longer friends at first, especially because besides Kaylin, Jaclyn used to be the only other friend who got the horse crazy thing.

Jaclyn glared at Emma until she passed by her, flipping her hair behind her shoulders as she sauntered down the hall. Emma groaned, opened the door the rest of the way and walked into the locker room. She tossed her bag on the ground and slumped onto the bench.

Melissa walked in a few minutes later and raised an eyebrow when she saw Emma with her palms on her cheeks.

"What's wrong?" Melissa asked.

"I just embarrassed myself in front of Jaclyn Alcott," Emma replied, her hands still covering her face.

Melissa gasped and slid next to Emma on the bench. "No way! How? I mean, it couldn't have been *that* bad."

"I smacked her in the face with the locker room door," Emma said, peeking through her hands to watch Melissa's reaction.

Melissa cringed. "Ouch. Yeah she's going to tell literally everyone at school about that one."

"I know!" Emma groaned. "How were we ever friends with her?"

"I mean, she wasn't so bad freshman and sophomore year. You know as well as I do that football boyfriend of hers was her downfall. Just like that, she was suddenly popular and had no time for people like *us*," Melissa said, rolling her eyes.

"This is exactly why boys are a waste of time," Emma thought. If a guy could turn Jaclyn into the rude, selfish person she had become, then Emma wanted nothing to do with them. She decided not to say it out loud for Melissa's sake. After all, Johnny was a nice enough boy, and he seemed to make Melissa happy.

"She won't be telling people *just* at school," Emma said breathlessly, suddenly realizing it wasn't the only place Jaclyn would surely be trash talking her.

Melissa's eyes widened. "What?"

"I have a show jumping competition in a week, and I *know* Jaclyn will be there. It's one she definitely wouldn't miss." Emma groaned again at the thought of Jaclyn running her mouth about Emma to anyone that would listen at the horse show.

Melissa shook her head. "Want me and Kaylin to come for moral support?" she asked.

"Yes! That would make it *less* painful," Emma replied.

"Good. I'm sure Kaylin was planning to go anyway. She can drive us since she has her driver's...," Melissa paused. "Oops. Sorry Em, I didn't mean to rub it in," Melissa added quickly, biting her bottom lip.

"It's ok, I know you didn't," Emma said, resting her hand on Melissa's shoulder.

"Did you reschedule your driving test again?" Melissa asked.

"Not yet. I think this time I'm going to wait until my dad's car is available."

There was no way she was going to attempt to back through cones in a minivan a second time.

Melissa offered a weak smile, still clearly feeling bad for Emma.

Emma smiled back at Melissa, and then thought of something to change the subject so her friend wouldn't feel guilty anymore.

"Did you bring your permission slip back for that class trip in two weeks?" Emma asked.

"I sure did! I'm so excited to go to Gibraltar Island. What about you?" Melissa asked.

"Me too! Spending two days with you and Kaylin away from school is always a good time," Emma replied.

Hopefully by then the drama between her and Jaclyn would be long forgotten. Emma tried not to think about being trapped on a six mile island in Lake Erie with Jaclyn still trying to make her life miserable.

Chapter Two

Emma took a deep breath and let it out slowly as she slid the saddle onto Lexington's back. Horse show nerves were in full swing now. It didn't matter how many times she showed, the nerves always seemed to find her. Lexington lipped at her pockets in search of treats, making Emma giggle.

"Sorry bud, you ate them all," Emma said, chuckling.

The announcer's voice echoed through the show barn, announcing her division was next. Butterflies in her stomach did backflips after the announcement. Emma tightened the girth and slid the bridle over the gelding's ears.

"Here goes nothing," she whispered, putting her helmet on her head and buckling the strap. Emma had managed to avoid Jaclyn and her friends when she checked in at the show office, and if she was lucky, maybe she could avoid seeing her the rest of the day. Or at the very least until she was done showing.

Emma led Lexington towards the mounting block that was just outside the show barn and swung her leg over the gelding's back. Maggie was already standing next to a jump in the warm-up ring waiting for her to arrive.

Emma waved to Maggie and asked Lexington to trot around the ring. After warming up sufficiently at the trot, Emma asked her horse to canter. Lexington cantered at a forward pace, and at seventeen hands, his large, open stride ate up the ground beneath them.

Lexington was the type of horse that Emma could always count on to be there when she needed him. He jumped bravely and put up with her silly antics when she wanted to gallop and jump around bareback. Maggie joked and called Lexington her babysitter. After all, Emma did get Lexington when she was only thirteen. After three years together, Emma and Lexington were a like a well-oiled machine when it came to jump courses.

A well-oiled machine that was about to be put to the test. Emma gasped, her jaw dropping as she witnessed Jaclyn Alcott and her horse enter the warm-up ring.

"*No!*" she thought. Why was Jaclyn in her division anyway? She had recently moved up a level. There was only one reason Jaclyn was entering her division today: to humiliate Emma.

Jaclyn's horse was a Warmblood with impeccable breeding. Her gelding came from a long line of incredibly talented jumpers. That talent had been passed down to her horse, Artemis.

Emma shuddered. Jaclyn's horse had to be one of the nicest horses, if not the nicest, at the show today. And Jaclyn knew it.

Jaclyn looked directly over at Emma, who had just asked Lexington to walk so she could catch her breath before taking the warm-up jumps. Emma's heart hammered in her chest as she thought about warming up in front of Jaclyn.

"Emma!" Maggie was waving over at her again. Other trainers were lining up next to the jump, waiting to have their own riders take it after Emma. It was now or never.

Emma took in a slow breath as she asked Lexington to canter forward. He jumped into the canter awkwardly, sensing his rider's tension. Emma tried to relax her body, remembering how Maggie always told her horses pick up on your emotions.

"Sorry, Lex," she murmured to her horse as she did a twenty-meter circle in front of the warm-up jump. She swallowed hard, feeling like every eye was on her. Jaclyn was halted at the other end of the warm-up ring staring directly at her still. Wasn't she supposed to be warming up too? Or be doing *anything* else besides staring at Emma?

There was no use stalling anymore. Jaclyn would probably have sat there staring at her if she did a hundred twenty meter circles. Emma put her leg on and pointed Lexington toward the cross rail in the center of ring. His ears pricked as he locked onto the jump. He took a studder step before the jump, chipping in before he jumped it awkwardly.

"Sorry," she apologized under her breath. Emma knew she should have added more leg before the jump. Her cheeks flushed red and she didn't dare look over at Jaclyn. Jaclyn's expression had surely turned smug.

"Come again, Emma! Keep him forward!" Maggie called out, setting the jump up to a vertical now.

Emma focused on the jump ahead of her and the horse under her. She pretended not to see Jaclyn who was still perfectly situated so that she was all Emma could see as she came into the fence.

"Focus!" she thought, her gaze drifting from Jaclyn to the announcer's booth in the distance instead.

Emma sent her horse forward, feeling the rhythm of his stride until he left the ground and they soared over the jump.

"Good, Emma, take it the other way and let's be done," Maggie instructed.

Emma circled her horse, feeling more confident now. Lexington jumped the now raised vertical again with ease. A smile stretched over her face, and she dared to turn back towards Jaclyn now.

But Jaclyn was cantering her horse around the warm-up ring, completely ignoring Emma.

"Figures," Emma mumbled to herself.

Walking her horse over to the main ring where she would be competing, Emma spotted Kaylin and Melissa leaning against the fence that surrounded the arena.

"Hey!" Emma called out to her friends who waved back and walked over to her.

"How was your warm-up?" Kaylin asked, patting Lexington's neck.

"Well, it was fine other than Jaclyn death glaring me ninety percent of the time," Emma said.

"Is she *seriously* starting trouble already? Just ignore her," Melissa replied, making a snorting sound in disgust.

"I'll try, but for whatever reason, she decided to enter *my* division."

"Didn't she move up a level?" Kaylin asked, wide-eyed.

"She did, but apparently she is bent on proving she is better than me in every way today," Emma replied, rolling her eyes and blowing out a breath.

"Try not to let her get to you," Kaylin said, shooting Emma a sympathetic look.

That, unfortunately, was easier said than done. Did she and Lexington even have a chance again Jaclyn and Artemis?

Emma stood next to her friends and chatted with them until it was time to head to the in-gate. For a moment, Emma was able get her mind off her impending rounds and Jaclyn. But the moment the announcer's voice stated they were beginning her division, her nerves came rushing back.

Emma clucked to Lexington and walked him towards the entry gate. As the first rider exited the arena, the announcer's voice rang out again. "Next in the ring is Jaclyn Alcott riding Artemis," he said.

Emma's heart sank.

"Great, now I have to ride directly after Jaclyn," she thought.

Jaclyn asked for the canter and Artemis stepped into a perfectly balanced, on-course pace. Emma fought the urge to roll her eyes knowing that would be bad sportsmanship. She typically encouraged and cheered on the other riders in her division but cheering for Jaclyn felt impossible. The best she could do was not let her face show the internal conflict she felt. And that conflict consisted of secretly hoping Artemis took a rail. Even if she knew it was wrong to wish that on anyone, including Jaclyn.

They had managed to make it around most of course now with a flawless round. No rails down and one glance at the timeclock let Emma know they were making good time in this power and speed jumper class.

She held her breath watching the pair land off the jump. "A clean round with a time of thirty point two seconds, putting this pair in the lead," the announcer said.

Maggie walked over to Emma from where she had been watching the round from the ring's fence line.

"You ready?" Maggie asked.

Emma gulped and nodded reluctantly. Lexington knew his job, she just needed to push Jaclyn from her mind and focus on her course.

She asked Lexington to go forward and through the in-gate into the arena.

"I can do this," Emma thought, trotting a circle as she waited for the buzzer.

But then, her eye caught a familiar face standing next to the in-gate and Jaclyn's horse. It was Luke Cromwell.

Emma felt her face go pale as she saw Luke chatting with Jaclyn's boyfriend, Chad. She knew they were friends, but why was *he* here?

"Emma! Go!" Kaylin's voice broke her train of thought. The buzzer had sounded and Emma was sitting there with her jaw slacked open. She slammed it shut and shortened her reins.

She asked Lexington for the canter and headed towards the first jump. He sailed over it with ease and jumped the next fence in the line just as easily. Emma tried to focus, but her mind kept drifting back to the in-gate. She just knew they were all staring at her, waiting for her to do something wrong.

It's funny how when you are so focused on doing something wrong, that that is exactly what you end up doing. Emma would later look back and wonder that if she had kept her focus, if things would have played out differently.

Emma cantered toward the blue striped jump ahead of her, clearing it with room to spare. But it was the moment she landed that she realized she didn't know where she was going next. It suddenly dawned on her that the reason she didn't know where to go next was because she had jumped the wrong jump.

"Rider off course. You are excused," the announcer said. Emma pulled Lexington to a walk and headed towards the gate. Heat flared in her cheeks as she waited for the gate to open in front of her. She didn't dare let her gaze fall on Luke, Jaclyn, and their friends, but she could hear the snickering from their direction anyway. Emma fought the tears welling in her eyes. Crying in front of them would only give them more ammo.

Emma beelined back to the show barn without saying a word to anyone.

She was mortified.

Emma was excited for this class trip to Gibraltar Island. That is, until she topped off her original embarrassment of hitting Jaclyn with the locker room door with forgetting her course at the horse show. Emma had given Jaclyn the exact tools she needed to potentially make the next few days for Emma completely miserable.

Hanging out on a six-mile island with all of your classmates should be fun. Unless of course, you're on Jaclyn's hit list.

The ferry that went from the Ohio mainland to the tiny island cut across the blue-green lake water. Emma watched as the reflecting sun's rays bounced off the water, remembering how her parents had taken her to several of the Lake Erie islands before. She always found herself forgetting she was still technically in her home state when she was here. It was like a tiny slice of northern paradise in the warmer months.

Jagged rock cliff formations could be seen around the edge of the island with greenery hanging over the sides of the cliffs as the ferry got closer to the island. Emma closed her eyes and smelled the lake water breeze coming off the side of the ferry. She promised herself not to let Jaclyn and her crew get to her while she was here. After all, it wasn't every day she got to have an island sleepover during school hours with her best friends.

"We're here!" Melissa squealed as the ferry began docking. A large, 1900's looking tan brick building covered in windows could be seen across from the dock. The rest of the island was hidden behind trees and plant life that lined the island's cliffs.

The students grabbed their gear and headed off the boat and onto the dock.

"This place is so cool!" Kaylin said, turning her head to take in the view. Students chatted in small groups excitedly around them.

"Ok everyone, we are going to have you drop your things off at your respective houses and we will meet back here at Stone Lab in twenty minutes!" their science teacher said, pointing to the tan brick building near the docks. "Ladies, you are in Harborview house at this end of the island," he said, pointing to the east side of the island. "And gentlemen, you're in Barney cottage across the island parallel to Harborview," the teacher said, pointing out the direction of the boys' housing. Students began running or jogging towards their respective houses before the teacher had finished his sentence completely.

"Twenty minutes!" the teacher's voice said again behind them.

Emma, Melissa, and Kaylin were already running full speed towards the Harborview house. "We are going to get the good beds for sure!" Melissa said breathlessly as they ran, peering behind her briefly to make sure they were far enough ahead to beat out most of the other girls.

Emma watched as trees and stunning glimpses of the cliff's drop-offs came in and out of view as they ran. She had to admit, this place was even more beautiful than she'd expected. Other than the few houses and the laboratory, the island still remained in its natural state, which was much different than the more populated islands on Lake Erie.

Only two other girls made it into the bunk house before they did. Melissa began checking out the house, looking for the perfect bed locations.

"Over here!" Melissa called out from the other room. Emma and Kaylin power-walked towards Melissa's voice. "In the corner, semi-private and near the windows," Melissa said proudly, motioning to the three beds she had claimed.

"Good choice," Kaylin agreed.

The three girls claimed their beds with their bags and then headed back outside. The house had started to get cramped with the other girls coming in to put their things away. They walked outside, staying close to the cliff's edge towards the docks.

"Oh look, a fire pit!" Melissa pointed out. It was directly on the water with wooden chairs around it.

"And a volleyball court!" Kaylin added as they continued down the path leading back to Stone Lab. Kaylin's parents were the school's volleyball coaches, so naturally she was on the team. Emma was sure she and Melissa would be forced to play later that evening whether they liked it or not.

They arrived back at the docks and the tan brick building with a few minutes to spare. Emma walked through the doors of the largest classroom in the lab and took their seats. She was glad that so far, she hadn't run into Jaclyn. But Emma knew it was only a matter of time.

"Welcome to Gibraltar Island, everyone!" one of Stone Lab's staff members said as the last of the students took their seats. The staff member told them the story of how the island came to be, and how it was now a private island used only for science research and teaching.

Emma found herself zoning out after the interesting stuff about the island was over and the actual learning began. She craned her head around slowly, and as nonchalantly as she could manage, until she caught sight of Jaclyn and her friends sitting in the last row of the classroom.

"Figures," she thought. She was glad they had chosen seats in the second row now. Kaylin had insisted they sit close since she actually enjoyed science. Emma loved nature and ecology, but some of the technical science type things reminded her of math, which of course, she was not so fond of.

For the next several hours, they learned about all kinds of things that were tied to the lake and the island. Emma found some of them to be more interesting than she'd expected. Still, she was glad when the learning was over and the evening free time began.

"Alright everyone, dinner is ready in the dining hall. After that, you can enjoy the island for the rest of the evening," the teacher said. Some of the students began dispersing in the direction of the dining hall. "Curfew is 9:00 pm!" the teacher called after them. Poor Mr. Moore. Emma was sure he would have his work cut out for him the next few days.

Kaylin put her hands on her hips and shot Melissa and Emma a look. "We *are* going to play volleyball after dinner, right?"

Melissa and Emma exchanged looks. "Of course Kay, we figured you would want to play," Melissa said, saying what Emma was already thinking. They headed to the dining hall and waited in the line of other students to get their buffet style dinner. That's when Emma saw Jaclyn, her boyfriend, Chad, and their friends ahead of them in line.

"Of course," Emma mumbled under her breath, sliding further behind the student in front of her. If she was lucky, maybe Jaclyn wouldn't spot her. Emma *knew* Jaclyn would find a way to publicly embarrass her, and so far, she had simply gotten lucky.

Melissa peered around the students in front of them until she caught sight of what had Emma so upset.

"Jaclyn," Melissa mouthed silently to Kaylin, who nodded, wide-eyed, shooting Emma a sympathetic look.

"Maybe she won't pull anything this time? I mean, maybe she will be distracted by all the fun tonight?" Kaylin whispered, half shrugging.

Sweet Kaylin. Always thinking the best of people. A trait Emma typically had as well, but when it came to Jaclyn, she knew better. Emma shot Kaylin a look that said she wasn't convinced.

"Remember what Jaclyn did the end of sophomore year?" Emma said. The incident sophomore year was the reason Jaclyn had officially crossed the line from former friend to enemy. Emma remembered standing by her locker, looking for a book for her next class when she felt a tugging on the back of her head. Reaching back to touch her hair, she had frozen the moment her fingers grazed the sticky piece of gum Jaclyn had lodged there.

Kaylin crinkled up her nose at the memory, and Kaylin's gaze dropped to the ground a moment. "Yeah, I remember."

"It was awful. Your mom had to cut a huge chunk of your hair out," Melissa said to Emma, frowning.

Emma placed her hand on Kaylin's shoulder. "Trust me, I wish it wasn't like this either, but Jaclyn has proven she capable of just about anything."

They were next in line to get their dinner now. Emma watched as Jaclyn and her friends finished piling food on their plates and then walked towards the tables in the far corner of the room near the windows.

"Well, at least I know where not to sit now," she thought.

Emma and her friends thanked the people serving the food and then headed to the opposite end of the dining hall. Emma tried to brush the bitter memories of Jaclyn from her mind and focus on her conversation with her friends.

"So I have been keeping a secret," Kaylin said, a grin stretched across her face. She seemed to be bursting at the seams.

"Spill!" Melissa said, leaning over the table. Emma leaned in too, waiting for Kaylin to speak again.

"I'm officially leasing a horse as of two days ago! I thought this trip would be a fun time to tell you guys," Kaylin said, beaming still.

"Kay! That's amazing news! I'm so happy for you," Emma gushed. She knew this was something Kaylin had wanted for a very long time. Emma understood what it was like to want a horse of your own so badly, and leasing one was the next best thing.

"I bet you are over the moon excited," Melissa chimed in, smiling warmly at Kaylin.

"I am," Kaylin said, her gaze meeting Melissa's, then Emma's.

"Tell me everything!" Emma pressed. Kaylin went on and on about the chestnut Quarter Horse mare, Winnie, she was now leasing. The girls made plans to visit Kaylin's barn and meet Winnie in the near future.

"Let's get to the volleyball court before it gets too crowded," Kaylin said, picking up her empty plate. Melissa and Emma exchanged a look and laughed at Kaylin's determination but picked up their plates and followed behind her anyway. Kaylin led the way out of the dining hall and across the grassy lawn towards the volleyball court.

A good sized group of their classmates were already gathering in the sand on either side of the net. Kaylin walked over to greet a couple of the girls who were on her volleyball team, and Melissa and Emma followed behind her.

A sudden feeling like someone punched her in the gut washed over Emma. Jaclyn, her friends, and Luke Cromwell stood in a group on the other side of the net from where Emma, Kaylin, and Melissa stood.

"Great," Emma mumbled. She had hoped Jaclyn would think she was too good for sand volleyball, but apparently Emma wasn't going to be that lucky. The icing on this cake of misery was that Luke appeared to be planning to play as well.

"Let's do boys against girls!" someone yelled out. Several other students called out in agreement.

"I like that idea!" Kaylin yelled out too, shooting an excited look at the girls from her volleyball team. Emma knew Kaylin meant well, but what her friend didn't know was that girls against boys meant she would have to be on the same team as Jaclyn. And what's more, in close proximity to her.

Perhaps Kaylin hadn't even noticed Jaclyn and her friends on the other side of the net. After all, she had been deep in conversation with her volleyball teammates. But, it was too late now. The boys were starting to move towards the opposite end of the court and the girls on the other side of the net were headed towards them, including Jaclyn. A smirk crossed Jaclyn's face when she spotted Emma.

Emma wished she could crawl under a rock, but Kaylin was already tugging at her arm and moving her into position on the court.

"This will be fu...," Kaylin cut herself off, now seeing Jaclyn duck under the net as she walked towards them. "Oops, sorry Em," Kaylin said, tossing Emma a sympathetic look.

What Emma didn't understand was, why her? Melissa and Kaylin were Jaclyn's friends too, but for some reason, she only had it out for Emma. Emma remembered racking her brain for anything she could have possibly done to cause Jaclyn to behave like this towards her. But to this day, she still had no idea why Jaclyn had made it her mission to make her miserable any chance she got.

Jaclyn stood only one person between Emma, Melissa, and Kaylin.

"Purposely, of course," Emma thought.

Luke stood directly in front of Emma on the other side of the volleyball net. Was he in on this too?

Emma swallowed hard; she just had to make it through one round of volleyball. Maybe after that she could pretend she twisted her ankle or something. But if she did, surely Jaclyn would be calling her a quitter or something just as vile.

Emma hoped all those times Kaylin made Emma and Melissa practice with her would pay off. Did Jaclyn even know how to play volleyball? Emma racked her brain for any information Jaclyn may have told her while they were still friends but came up with nothing. Maybe that was a good thing. Maybe that meant Emma just might have the upper hand this time...

"Serving!" the boy across the net said, pulling her from her thoughts as he launched the volleyball across the net directly towards Emma.

"Got it!" Kaylin called out, practically diving in front of Emma, sending the ball back over the net.

"*Pay attention!*" Emma's brain screamed. Embarrassing herself in front of Jaclyn, Luke, and half her class wouldn't help her situation. The volleyball went back and forth over the net several more times before it came Emma's way again.

"Yours, Em!" Kaylin's voice said behind her.

Emma crouched down, getting under the ball like she had been taught and sent the ball back over the net. A smile tugged at the corners of her lips. Maybe she would make it through this game with minimal embarrassment after all.

One of Kaylin's teammates served the ball and aced it on the first try, tying up the game.

"Looks like we are going to beat those boys!" Kaylin whispered to Emma and Melissa, a devious smile on her face.

It was the boys' serve this time, and the ball came flying over the net towards Emma once again. Emma took two steps forward anticipating where the ball was going to land. But suddenly, she felt her feet come out from under her and found herself falling face first into the sand. What had she tripped over? There had been nothing in her way!

Then, it hit her; it was Jaclyn. She had been standing incredibly close right before Emma starting walking towards the ball. Had she really tripped her own teammate just to embarrass Emma?

Loud laughter from the boys' side of the net and a few of the girls, presumably Jaclyn and her friends, echoed through the air as Emma peeled herself off the ground. Dusting sand off her body, she felt her cheeks flush red.

"Looks like volleyball isn't the only thing you aren't coordinated enough to do," Jaclyn chided.

"What is *that* supposed to mean?" Emma said, her face scrunching up as she felt heat creep up her neck.

"Oh nothing, just that *all* sports seem to not be your thing," Jaclyn added, a venomous look was in her eyes. It was obvious to Emma what she was referring to: the horse show.

Emma felt her jaw drop but slammed it shut. A hundred mean things she could say to Jaclyn entered her mind. She opened her mouth, ready to tell Jaclyn exactly what she was thinking but stopped herself at the last moment. Emma wasn't Jaclyn, and behaving like her would only mean she was stooping to her level.

Emma said nothing but turned and began walking off the volleyball court.

"Seriously, Jaclyn?" a boy's voice reprimanded her from the other side of the net said. It sounded a lot like Luke's. Why would Luke defend her against Jaclyn? He was friends with Jaclyn's boyfriend, Chad, after all. Emma shot a quick glance to the other said of the net and saw Luke shaking his head, looking in Jaclyn's direction. Emma tried not to read too much into it as she grabbed her shoes from the side of the court and headed away from the volleyball net.

"Wait up!" Melissa's voice said behind her. She heard two sets of footfalls on the grass behind her but didn't stop walking until she was far enough away from the volleyball court that she couldn't see or hear anything else Jaclyn was surely saying.

Emma stood by the edge of one of the island's cliffs. The only sound she could hear was the waves crashing against the rocks below. She took a deep breath, letting it out slowly and turned around to face her friends. "Kaylin, go back to the volleyball court. I know how badly you wanted to play. I'll be fine," Emma said, forcing a smile.

"But Em...," Kaylin began.

"I'll stay with her, but Emma's right, you've been looking forward to this all day. Go show Jaclyn what a real volleyball player looks like," Melissa added with a wink.

"Are you sure?" Kaylin asked, still looking like she felt bad for doing so.

"Go!" Emma said, playfully pushing Kaylin towards the volleyball court, smiling broader to reassure her.

"Ok, I'll come find you guys after the game," Kaylin said, taking a few reluctant steps away from her friends.

"See you!" Melissa said, looping her arm through Emma's as she led her the opposite direction.

"What is *wrong* with that girl?" Melissa said, shaking her head as they walked along the jagged cliffs. "I'm sorry Jaclyn did that to you," Melissa added, offering a sympathetic smile.

"It's ok, I'm used to it by now," Emma said, rolling her eyes.

Would this feud between them ever end?

Chapter Three

Melissa squealed as the marshmallow at the end of her stick caught on fire. Emma laughed, watching as Melissa struggled to blow the flame out of her now scorched marshmallow.

"There goes another one," Melissa said, tossing it into her mouth anyway and opening the marshmallow bag to get a new one.

"Maybe you should try keeping them further away from the flames this time?" Emma suggested, chuckling under her breath.

"But I like them a little extra toasted," Melissa replied with a shrug, popping the new marshmallow onto her stick.

"I wouldn't say burnt to a crisp is a little extra toasted. At this rate, you're never going to make a full s'more," Emma said, laughing.

Melissa shrugged. "The best part of the s'more is the marshmallows anyway."

Melissa put her marshmallow dangerously close to the flames once more. The fire flickered in the pit in front of them, and the light from the flames made the water beside them glisten. In Emma's opinion, it was the prettiest spot on the island at night.

It had been a lovely rest of the evening despite how it started. Melissa and Emma ran into Mr. Moore shortly after the volleyball court incident, and he offered them s'more supplies and said he was setting up a fire. Emma remembered the firepit that sat at the water's edge and figured it would be a good place to hide out and enjoy the rest of the night on the island.

A few other classmates joined them, and luckily for Emma, none of them were Jaclyn or her friends. Kaylin was still playing volleyball and Emma was glad the incident hadn't kept Kaylin from enjoying herself.

"I'm going to find the restroom," Emma said, standing up and stretching. She walked up the rocky path towards steps that led up to the top of the cliff and squinted her eyes in the darkness. Crickets chirped as she walked along in the dim light of the full moon. Finally, a lamp post next to the bathrooms could be seen in the distance.

"Emma?" a male voice said, and footfalls could be heard to her left.

Emma paused, recognizing the voice. "Luke?"

"Yeah, it's me," he said, stepping into the low light.

Emma tilted her head, surprised he was even talking to her. She peered around him just to be safe. None of his buddies were nearby. Emma racked her brain for the last time she saw Luke without his friends at his heels. She was pretty sure the answer was never.

"I hope you're ok. Sorry about earlier...," he began, his gaze dropping to the ground. He looked like he meant it.

"I'm fine. But thanks anyway," Emma replied, her words ringing with surprise. Why he was apologizing to her about anything was strange enough...let alone on Jaclyn's behalf.

Luke looked back up, meeting her gaze. He opened his mouth like he was going to say something else, but didn't.

Emma started walking towards the bathroom building again.

"Don't trip on your way to the bathroom," another voice said behind her.

Ah, there they were. Luke's friends. Right on time.

Emma rolled her eyes as she turned around, biting her tongue to keep herself from telling those boys to walk off a cliff.

"Don't you have *anything* better to do?" Emma said instead. It wasn't nearly as satisfying as the other things she wanted to say.

Before she could give them the chance to come up with what would surely be a lame follow up response, she turned on her heels towards the bathroom building and powerwalked away from the cackling boys.

Emma spent a little extra time in the bathroom building, craning around the corner to make sure she wouldn't have to deal with Luke and his annoying friends on her way back to the fire pit. When she finally made it back to the fire, Kaylin was sitting next to Melissa.

"Kay! How was volleyball?" Emma asked, taking a seat next to her friends.

"So much fun! We ended up beating the boys, of course," Kaylin said proudly. "It would have been more fun with you guys though.

"I'm glad you took those boys down for us. Was Jaclyn on better behavior after Emma and I left?" Melissa asked.

"Well, she and a couple of her friends just walked off the court not long after you and Emma left," Kaylin replied.

Go figure. Was Jaclyn only playing in hopes of using it to publicly humiliate her? Not that Emma was surprised. She knew Jaclyn would find some way to get back at her after hitting her with the locker room door. Jaclyn always had to have the last laugh.

The girls sat around the fire and talked for a while longer.

Kaylin yawned widely. "What time is it anyway?"

Melissa checked her watch. "Almost nine, actually."

Was it really curfew already?

"That's ok, I'm beat anyway. You two ready to head back to the house?" Kaylin said.

Emma nodded as she stood up and Melissa followed suit. They made their way up the stairs and walked along the cliff's edge, peering out at the lake now and then that shined in the light of the moon.

"I don't want to leave this place!" Melissa whispered as they walked along.

"It is pretty," Kaylin added.

They reached the entrance of the house and tiptoed in. Many of the others were already asleep. Melissa led the way back toward where their beds were but stopped short with a gasp. Emma saw what had made Melissa gasp; three other girls were sleeping in the beds they had claimed.

"Guess we are sleeping somewhere else," Kaylin said, frowning. "Where are our bags?" Emma whispered, noticing they weren't anywhere on the ground in this room at all. Melissa shot her a concerned look and then turned on her heels as she began searching the house for their things.

"Em, Kaylin!" Melissa whispered the other room. They tiptoed over to find their things slumped in a corner far away from any of the beds. There was really only one person who would be rude enough to do something like this.

"Jaclyn," Emma hissed under her breath.

Melissa walked over to the last three beds that had not yet been claimed. "Umm, we have a problem."

Emma and Kaylin leaned in to see what Melissa was looking at.

"That's disgusting," Kaylin said, staring at the pile of vomit on one of the beds.

Emma sighed. It looked like one of them wasn't going to be sleeping on a bed tonight.

"You guys take the beds. My dad has taken us tent camping every summer since I was three," Emma said, offering a half smile to her friends.

"Em…," Melissa began.

"I'll be fine. One of us has to sleep on the ground, so it may as well be me," Emma said, gathering her pillow and other bedding.

Before her friends could protest, Emma hugged them both. "I'll see you in the morning."

"Where are you going?" Kaylin asked.

"I would rather sleep on the soft grass than on the dirty hard floor of the house," Emma said.

Melissa and Kaylin shot her a somber look, but Emma smiled as warmly as she could before turning towards the front door.

The night air was cool and the waves crashing against the edges of the island sounded like a natural lullaby to Emma. She found a spot that was tucked away so that Jaclyn wouldn't see her. The last thing Emma wanted was to give Jaclyn the pleasure of seeing her sleeping on the ground, no thanks to her meddling.

Emma took a deep breath and laid her blanket on the ground, pulling the other one over her legs. It was a nice night, at least.

Emma wished she hadn't been right about Jaclyn turning this trip into a way to get back at her. But unfortunately, she had.

Emma looked up at the cloudless sky, letting the sun's rays warm her face.

The smell of the air let her know that spring was in full swing and her favorite season of all, summer, was on its way.

Something about days like this made riding her horse that much better. Emma needed a good day after the not so perfect last few days she had on the Gibraltar Island class trip. Not that it had been *all* bad. She did have a good time with her friends despite Jaclyn's attempts to make her miserable.

Natalie, one of the other riders at the barn, was already in the outdoor arena mounting up. Emma waved to her barn friend as she walked towards the mounting block with the tacked up Lexington in tow behind her.

"Hi Emma! I didn't know you would be out here today!" Natalie said warmly. Today's perfect weather seemed to be making everyone that much happier.

"I wasn't sure I would be able to, but luckily my mom had time to drop me off before she ran errands," Emma replied. It was yet another reminder that she needed to pass her driving test before she was finally able to have the freedom to drive herself to the barn.

Emma brushed off the unpleasant reminder and focused on her horse. Swinging her leg over Lexington's back, she clucked him forward into the walk.

Emma and Natalie chatted as they warmed up. Emma told Natalie about the week she'd had and the class trip she'd taken.

"This Jaclyn sounds awful," Natalie said, frowning as they walked their horses side by side now.

"You have no idea," Emma replied.

"At least Luke stood up for you," Natalie said.

Emma shot Natalie a look that said she wasn't convinced. "Luke didn't exactly stand up for me. I mean, he may have made a comment to Jaclyn...," Emma trailed off, shaking her head. "But Luke's annoying friends laughed and made comments, and Luke said nothing to them," Emma said, feeling quite certain she had made her point.

"I guess not," Natalie said, frowning.

Still, Emma wondered if Natalie had a hard time seeing Luke the way she did: for who he really was. Every teenage girl at the barn had a crush on him, as did most of the girls at her school. Emma remembered late last year when Natalie told her how jealous she was that Emma went to school with Luke. Emma had laughed, thinking she was joking at first. But Natalie had been dead serious.

It was funny how things seemed to be changing since she turned sixteen. She noticed it happening with all her friends at school and even Natalie who was her age but attended a different high school. It was like someone turned on some sort of boy crazy switch in everyone's brains. Still, Emma didn't see the appeal.

Emma asked Lexington to canter. There was only one thing that was going to get her mind off of how annoying Luke was: jumping. Emma wondered if there was another feeling in the world that felt the way it did to fly through the air on the back of a horse.

The first time she ever jumped was burned in her brain forever. Nerves, excitement, fear, and the thrill of flying were all mixed up inside her those few seconds between leaving the ground and being airborne.

It's why Emma wondered how Natalie could ever want to waste time with boys when she could be riding. Ever since she got a boyfriend, Emma had noticed Natalie wasn't at the barn nearly as much as she used to be. What was all the hype about anyway? It certainly couldn't feel like this, like jumping.

Emma pointed Lexington toward the first jump, a cross rail, letting him stretch out as he took it with ease. Emma smiled; there was *definitely* nothing better than this.

Emma brought Lexington back to the walk for a moment and Natalie trotted over to them.

"Speak of the devil," Natalie whispered, eyeing Emma and then the other end of the arena.

There, arms hanging over the fence line, was Luke Cromwell. Emma fought the urge to roll her eyes. She had no interest in her ride being ruined by Luke's prying eyes the entire time.

"Maybe if we ignore him he will go away," Emma murmured back.

"Whatever, he's cute. He can watch us ride if he wants," Natalie said, waving in Luke's direction. Luke waved back at Natalie and then his gaze landed on Emma.

Emma accidentally locked eyes with him. She paused, not wanting to give him the wrong idea. But if she simply looked away, that would be incredibly rude considering Natalie had just been so overly friendly. She may not like Luke, but she did like being able to work off her horse's board at his family's farm.

Emma offered him a half smile and a quick wave. Luke's eyes widened and a warm smile spread across his face. Emma looked away quickly after that. Perhaps he was simply that surprised she had made any sort of friendly gesture. The last time she checked, it was the first time she had ever done so.

"He isn't completely awful when he's alone, but the moment his friends are involved, he's just as bad as they are," she reminded herself. And when weren't they around?

As if on cue, Emma heard boys' voices from across the way, near Luke's house.

"Come on, Luke!" one friend called out. They were clearly waiting on him. Why was he out here anyway?

"Coming!" Luke said, turning and jogging back toward the house.

"Typical," she thought. Always doing exactly what his friends wanted him to do.

"He is *so* cute," Natalie gushed after he walked away.

Emma resisted the urge to say something rude about Luke to Natalie. After all, it was clear he could do no wrong in her eyes.

"Want to do some jump courses with me?" Emma asked, changing the subject. She was already sick of talking about Luke.

"Sure!" Natalie said, looking excited and peeling her eyes from Luke who was still jogging towards his friends in the distance.

At least there was still one thing that seemed to hold Natalie's interest slightly above boys.

For now, anyway.

Emma checked her watch one more time.

There was no way the bus was this late, which could only mean one thing: it came early and left without her.

Groaning, she picked her backpack up off the ground where she had let it fall a few minutes ago. With all the books she needed to take home from school today, it became heavy rather quickly.

Kaylin and Melissa left a long time ago and were probably home by now. Both her parents worked late tonight, which meant she was stuck at school for who knows how long.

Well, if she was going to be stuck here, she definitely wasn't going to stand next to the bus stop for however long it took for someone to come get her.

With her driver's test rescheduled for two days from now, it felt a little bit ironic that today of all days she would miss the bus. Especially considering she hadn't missed it once this year so far.

Emma trudged back towards the school, wondering where she should wait. It didn't actually seem all that appealing to sit inside on such a nice day. Instead, she found herself headed towards one of the picnic tables that sat close to the side of the building next to the student parking lot. Luckily, it wasn't raining like it had been the last two days.

Emma tossed her backpack on one of the seats of the table. Stepping up onto the table part, she laid her back against the cool wood and folded her hands across her chest, her feet planted and her knees in the air. Maybe if she was lucky she could get a base tan out of it at the very least.

Closing her eyes, she listened to the sounds of birds and the last of the students starting their cars in the parking lot.

"Must be nice," she thought. Emma had been farm or pet sitting any chance she got so she could save up enough money to buy her first car once she got her driver's license. With just over $1,000 saved, she hoped to find something that ran well enough to get her to school, the barn, and back. That was really her only criteria. Although, she did have these daydreams about driving around with the sunroof open, the wind blowing her hair...

"Emma?" a voice said, pulling her from her thoughts. Her eyes snapped open and she turned her head to match the face with the familiar voice. The pick-up truck with his farm's logo was unmistakable.

Of course, it would be none other than Luke Cromwell. Just her luck. Emma sat up and did a quick scan of the parking lot for his annoying friends who always seemed to make her blood boil.

Emma's eyes met Luke's. He had one eyebrow raised curiously.

"Oh, hey," she mumbled. Why was he at school so late anyway?

Luke tilted his head, eyeing her curiously. "What are you doing?"

Emma shrugged. "I missed the bus so I'm waiting for someone to pick me up."

"Yeah that used to happen to me all the time before I started driving to school." Luke replied, a smile tugging at his lips.

"Of course it did," Emma thought.

"I don't normally miss the bus," Emma added quickly, making sure Luke knew she was nothing like him. She figured it would probably be overkill to mention it was the first time in over a year she had missed the bus.

Luke laughed casually. "I don't doubt that."

"What does *that* mean?" Emma said, a little bit of defensiveness was creeping into her tone now.

"Just that you're a good girl," Luke replied, shrugging.

Emma felt heat flush in her cheeks. "A *good* girl?" Emma repeated. Her tone even more defensive this time.

Luke's eyes widened. "I didn't mean it as a bad thing."

Emma's held Luke's gaze, her eyes narrowed. She wasn't so sure about that.

"So, how much longer until your ride arrives?" Luke asked.

"Well, no one is actually on their way yet. My parents are still at work for at least another hour or so," Emma replied.

"Want me to give you a ride home? Or to the barn at least? I do live there after all," Luke said, flashing her a brilliant smile. Emma paused, wondering why his smile was making her thoughts fuzzy.

"Um, I don't know..," Emma stammered. It went against everything she felt about Luke to accept a ride from him. Could she stand being trapped in a car with him for fifteen whole minutes?

"Come on, it beats sitting on this bench for another couple hours," Luke said, holding her gaze.

Emma weighed the pros and cons in her mind. It *would* be nice not to have to sit in the school parking lot for hours. Seeing her horse instead of sitting here would be an added bonus, and then Luke wouldn't be driving her out of the way to her house. She didn't want to owe Luke any favors. She supposed it wouldn't be so bad to tolerate close proximity to him for the next fifteen minutes if he was simply driving her to the barn, since he was going there anyway.

Emma blew out a breath and picked up her backpack off the ground.

"Ok, I guess catching a ride with you to the barn would be nice. You know, since it's not out of your way. Thanks," Emma said, forcing herself to smile politely at Luke. It still felt strange that he had even offered her a lift at all, but she supposed even guys like Luke could have moments where they weren't completely awful.

"You're welcome," Luke said, hopping out of the driver's side quickly to open the door for Emma on the passenger side.

Emma's eyes widened in surprise. She hadn't expected Luke to open the door for her. Maybe his parents had taught him manners after all?

Emma tossed her backpack in the back of the truck and climbed into the passenger seat. Luke made his way back to the driver's side and turned up the radio before putting the truck in gear.

"You like country music?" Emma asked. She couldn't help herself. He just didn't seem like type to enjoy that kind of music, especially considering the type of music that could be heard blaring from all of Luke's friends' cars when they left the school parking lot.

"Don't tell me you don't like country music. Otherwise, you will be finding your own way home again," Luke teased, winking her way.

"Are you kidding? I love country music! I just didn't think *you* did," Emma said, surprising herself with the enthusiasm in her tone.

"I grew up listening to a lot of 90's country. My mom played it constantly in the barn, around the house...," Luke trailed off, his gaze dropped to the steering wheel a moment and he cleared his throat. Emma thought he looked uncomfortable for some reason.

Luke turned toward Emma again. "Anyway, it's what I was raised on, and it's been my favorite type of music ever since."

Emma realized she had never seen Luke's mom in the barn. In fact, no one ever mentioned her at all, come to think about it. Maybe she lost interest in horses at some point? It seemed impossible to have never met Luke's mother even once though, especially since Emma had been riding at Luke's family farm for over three years. To never have seen his mom once in three years was beyond strange. Emma considered pressing him for details but decided against it.

What did it matter to her anyway? She and Luke weren't even friends. Less than friends, actually.

A thick silence fell between them as they drove down the back roads towards the farm.

"I heard about what Jaclyn did at the Gibraltar Island trip. Sorry she made you sleep on the ground," Luke said, shooting Emma a sympathetic look.

Great, so people *had* found out about that. And if Luke knew, at least half of her junior class knew too.

"It's fine, I grew up tent camping," Emma said, shrugging. Luke was apologizing for Jaclyn's actions? Was she in the twilight zone or something? Maybe he just didn't have anything better to say to her and wanted to break the silence.

Luke half smiled, then focused his attention back on the road and tapped his thumb on the steering wheel to the song playing.

A few minutes later they were pulling into the driveway of the barn. The white fences with white oak trees lining the driveway blurred by on either side of the truck as it rumbled down the gravel drive.

"Thanks for the ride," Emma said, turning to face Luke. She did actually appreciate the gesture, although somehow she still found herself suspicious of it.

"Anytime, if you miss the bus again...," Luke began.

Emma held up her hand, cutting him off. "Oh that will *not* be happening again. Plus, I have my driving test rescheduled for a few days from now, so hopefully I'll be driving myself to school soon."

Emma hoped she made it clear this situation was a one off.

"Rescheduled?" Luke asked, his head tilting a little with curiosity.

Emma felt her cheeks flush. "Yeah, I took the test in my mom's minivan the first time and failed the cone parallel parking portion."

Luke let out a deep, genuine laugh. Emma instinctively felt defensive and opened her mouth to tell him off, or at the very least make him realize just how hard it was to take the driver's test in a van.

"I did the exact same thing! Except, I used my dad's old pick-up that had a truck bed topper, the kind that comes all the way up to the top of the back window. It was *impossible* to see out the back of it. I blasted through an entire line of cones the first time I took my test," Luke said.

Despite herself, Emma found herself laughing right along with Luke. "I made sure to borrow my dad's car for this test. Failing your driving test is mortifying," she said.

Emma realized she was still holding Luke's gaze and smiling. What was she doing? Fraternizing with the enemy? She cleared her throat and dropped her gaze.

She pulled her backpack from the back seat of the truck. "Well, um...anyway, thanks for again for the ride," Emma stammered.

"You're welcome," Luke replied.

Emma decided not to look back over at him this time. She and Luke were not friends, and tomorrow when they were roaming the school hallways she was sure he and his friends would act exactly like they always did...which was pretending like she didn't exist. Or worse, they endlessly tormented her alongside Jaclyn.

Emma slid out of the truck and shut the door behind her. She could still feel Luke staring at her though. As casually as she could manage, she looked over her shoulder and offered a halfhearted wave as an excuse to look back at him. Luke was still smiling warmly and waved back.

"What just happened?" she thought as she headed toward Lexington's stall.

It was certainly the oddest encounter she ever had with Luke Cromwell. Maybe he happened to be bearable without his entourage of annoying friends. That, however, was exactly the problem. Other than this one incident, they were practically inseparable. Not to mention one of Luke's closest friends was Jaclyn's boyfriend, her now sworn enemy.

There was just no world where she and Luke could be friendly, let alone friends. Today had been anomaly, she was sure of it.

"You are the only man I could ever truly love," Emma whispered to Lexington, who hung is head out of his stall lazily. She ran her hand up his forelock, twisting the hair around with her fingers.

A smile stretched over her face. Horses were the only thing that truly made any sense to her in this world.

Chapter Four

Emma stuffed her regular school clothes in a bag and shoved them into a gym locker.

Melissa stood near the door of the locker room waiting on her.

"I don't know about you, but I'm excited for dodgeball day," Melissa said, a grin stretched across her face.

Emma laughed. "You say that every time we play this game in gym class."

"What? I mean how often do you get a chance to launch balls at your fellow classmates? Especially the ones you don't like," Melissa replied.

Melissa had a point. Emma would love nothing more than to launch a ball directly at Jaclyn's head. Too bad head shots were off limits. At least, if she didn't want to be sidelined the rest of the game. Although, it seemed like it might actually be worth it this time.

Emma let out a slightly devious chuckle. "You know what Melissa, I think I might just be excited about dodgeball today too."

Emma and Melissa walked into the school's gym. The other students were gathered in small groups talking with one another. A loud, sharp whistle interrupted everyone's conversations.

"Ok, lets pick teams!" Mr. Jay, the gym teacher, said.

Several hands flew up immediately, vying for a chance to be picked as captain.

"Alright, Chad and Luke, you can be captains this time," Mr. Jay said. Both boys had been begging Mr. Jay for the last few weeks to be captain and it seemed like today, Mr. Jay was out of reasons not the let them. He *had* to know the consequences of letting those two yahoos be captains. Perhaps that's why he had waited so long to break down and choose them in the first place.

The glimmer of excitement dodgeball had presented in the locker room was quickly vanishing. Emma and Melissa weren't exactly first pick material. Although, Emma had always taken offense to that. After all, she was a horse girl. She rode one thousand pound animals and yet no one seemed to remember that when it was time to play a team sport.

"Whatever, maybe I can at least blast Jaclyn with a dodgeball if I'm lucky enough to end up on the opposite team," she thought.

"Scotty!" Luke called out, pointing to the boy standing near the front of the group of students that had gathered in front of the two team captains.

"Jaclyn!" Chad called out, pointing and winking to his girlfriend.

Typical. Of course Chad would pick his own girlfriend first. The worst part was that she wasn't any more qualified or better at dodgeball than Emma. Especially considering the only sport she and Jaclyn did was horseback riding.

Melissa looked over at Emma and rolled her eyes. Emma pressed her lips together to hold in a laugh at Melissa's expression which reflected her own thoughts.

The two boys continued to call out names of their classmates as their teams began filling up. Emma crossed her arms over her chest. She and Melissa were among the last of the students left to be picked.

"Felix," Chad said, but the enthusiasm had left his tone about seven students ago.

"Melissa," Luke called out. Emma felt her jaw drop and immediately slammed it shut. Well, it figured. She had been right about Luke after all. Emma wondered why for a split second she thought that maybe Luke would pick her. It was stupid, really. She already knew nothing would change between them just because they spent fifteen minutes trapped in a truck together. Sure, Melissa ran track her freshman year, but that was two years ago.

Emma all but stomped over to Chad's team. No use in giving him the satisfaction of calling her name. She was the last one standing; of course she was on his team.

"Great, now not only am I on a different team than Melissa, but I'm on the same team as Jaclyn. Looks like there would be no consolation prize of blasting Jaclyn in the face with any balls today," she thought.

Melissa mouthed a "sorry" from the other side of the gym. Emma offered a half-hearted smile in response. It wasn't Melissa's fault Luke picked her before Emma.

"Ok, Chad's team, this side! Luke's, this side!" Mr. Jay yelled above the chatting students, pointing to the respective sides. The students of each team made their way to their respective sides of the gym. A line of dodgeballs was already lined up across the center line of the gymnasium.

Emma crouched down, waiting for the whistle. Well, it may not be Jaclyn, but maybe one of Luke's annoying friends would be a decent dodgeball target. Or maybe even Luke himself.

A sharp whistle pulled her from her thoughts. Emma used all her strength to sprint towards the line of balls, grabbing one and hurdling it towards the most annoying of Luke's friends. He saw it coming at the last second and swerved out of the way.

"Shoot!" Emma thought, picking a ball off the ground and swerving out of the way of one launched at her almost simultaneously.

Dodgeballs flew back and forth from either side and students squealed as the balls made contact. Emma watched as Melissa walked reluctantly off the gym floor after a ball grazed her right leg.

It was only Emma and three other students left on her team now. On Luke's team, six remained. Emma felt a slight smirk cross her face knowing she had made it this long. Maybe Luke would rethink the next time he decided to pick everyone else but her for his team. Not that she cared about Luke picking her, of course. It would just be nice not to be picked at the end next time...

A ball sped past her ear, making a whistling sound and she swerved at the last second. Emma felt her eyes widen. The speeding bullet of a dodgeball sent her way had come from none other than Luke Cromwell.

"This means *war*," Emma mumbled under her breath, picking a dodgeball off the ground. Emma launched the ball back at Luke using every bit of strength she had left. Luke leaped out of the way, a devious smile on his face, quickly picking another ball off the ground and sending it back towards Emma. They fired off three more rounds at each other back and forth, with Emma barely making it out of the way of the ball each time. Meanwhile, Luke seemed to effortlessly sidestep his way out of every ball Emma threw.

"How is he making it look so easy?" she thought.

Luke picked up the ball Emma had just thrown, raising the ball up behind his head, throwing it even harder this time. Emma started to duck down, but it was too late. The ball smacked into her forehead causing a pinging sound as it bounced off her face. She lost her balance and fell backward on the hard, wooden gym floor.

Emma saw stars as she waited for her vision to return to normal. "Ow!" she said, sitting up, her palm on her forehead. She heard the sound of several sneakers running towards her.

"Emma, are you alright?" Mr. Jay asked. Melissa was on his heels and crouched down next to Emma.

"I'm fine," Emma said, feeling more embarrassed than in pain.

"Emma, I'm *so* sorry. I wasn't aiming for your head, I...," Luke began, hovering over her now.

Emma waved her hand in the air, stopping him mid-sentence. "Oh sure you weren't Luke." Venom was dripping in her words.

Ugh! Like she hadn't had enough embarrassing moments this year. Summer couldn't come quick enough. Not that it would help her Luke problem since he and his buddies just *loved* to roam the barn aisles like they had nothing better to do.

"Come on Emma, let's get you to the nurse's office," Mr. Jay said, helping her up. Emma shot one last glance of distain towards Luke before she stood up and turned her back on him.

Well, it was official. Even dodgeball had been ruined by Luke Cromwell.

Emma swung her leg over Lexington's bare back, grabbing a little mane as she steadied herself. She patted his dark neck and smiled down at him. His ears were pricked in the direction of the open pasture gate in front of them. After the terrible day she had had yesterday, Emma knew this might just be the only thing that could help her forget.

Her head hadn't hurt nearly as much as her pride by the end of the day. Surely Jaclyn and her friends had been snickering in the corner the moment the dodgeball had made contact with her face. Emma could only imagine the word, "karma" had escaped Jaclyn's lips, claiming it was somehow retribution from when Emma hit her with the locker room door. Like she hadn't made Emma pay for that already.

Emma shook her head, clearing her mind of yesterday's problems. Right now, she was in her happy place: at the barn with her horse.

She clucked to him, asking him to step forward and through the open pasture cate. The back pasture was her favorite place to ride, especially bareback. The feeling of freedom as her horse cantered openly through the soft grass and endless acres of land back here might just be enough to wash away her troubles at school. At least for a little while, anyway.

Lexington plodded along, his ears swiveling as he took in the scenery around them. Emma was thankful for a horse like Lex; he was the best horse any girl could ask for.

The one other bright spot about today was that Emma had taken her driver's test again, and this time she had passed. That meant no more missing the bus, and what's more, now she could drive herself to the barn. When her mother had handed her the keys to the minivan and said to come right back after the barn, Emma's heart sang.

Perhaps the worst parts of this school year were behind her. It could only go up from here, right?

Emma clucked to Lexington again, and he stepped into a smooth, medium paced trot. He had a large stride, but one that was floaty enough that riding him bareback was still comfortable. He seemed just a little more careful with his pace when she was riding bareback. Sometimes she swore her horse read her mind.

After trotting down the long side of the fence, Emma reached the pasture's edge. Lexington shook his head, and she could feel his muscles bunching up under her. She laughed at his antics; he knew exactly what she was about to ask of him.

"Ok bud, let's go!" Emma said, wrapping her fingers through a chunk of mane and giving him a gentle squeeze. Lexington went from a dead stop to an open canter instantly. Emma beamed as the former racehorse ate up the ground, now galloping towards the other end of the pasture.

This was Emma and Lexington's favorite thing to do when they needed a break from regular arena riding. His hooves pounded and the wind whistled past her ears as they galloped on. Lexington may be in his late teens now, but when she let him stretch his legs and gallop out in the pastures, it was like he was a three year old back on the racetrack again. Emma wondered if he felt as alive as she did. Based on his reaction, she had a feeling he did.

Emma laughed at her horse's reaction when she asked him to slow down as she neared the other end of the pasture.

"We will do this again soon, I promise," she murmured. Emma walked Lexington out for a long time, enjoying the feeling of the spring sun on her skin. After a long, cold winter of riding inside, the sun just seemed to hit her a little differently for those first few months of nicer weather. Nothing compared to riding outside, in her opinion.

Emma headed towards the pasture's gate as they wrapped up their ride. It looked like, however, her school troubles were going to follow her even to her happiest place. Luke was leaned against the wood pole at the entrance of the pasture, his arms folded across his chest, a slight smirk tugging at his lips. Emma felt her blood begin to boil. Why was he standing there watching her ride? Hadn't he done enough damage already?

"Hey, Emma," Luke said when she was close enough to hear him. There was no avoiding walking past him, unfortunately. It was no coincidence he had chosen to stand directly in the path of her only exit.

Emma tried to avoid eye contact as she steered her horse through the small gap between Luke and the open gate.

"He'll move if he doesn't want to get run over," she thought. Secretly, she hoped he didn't move.

Luke looked wide-eyed at Emma as she proceeded to pass by him without a word. "Em, please, I'm trying to apologize here...," Luke began.

Emma spun around to meet his gaze, her eyes narrowed. "Don't call me Em. That term is reserved for my actual friends," she said. Emma turned back around and clucked Lexington on. If she had to trot the rest of the way back to the barn, she would.

"Emma, come on!" Luke pleaded. Emma thought she heard a hint of sincerity in his voice.

"Don't fall for it," she reminded herself. As far as she could tell, Luke *meant* to blast her in the face with the ball.

Finally Luke seemed to be tired of jogging after her, and the next time Emma glanced over her shoulder as she approached the barn, he was stopped in his tracks quite a ways back.

Good riddance. She didn't need Luke or his apologies. And she certainly didn't need his pity, or whatever his angle was.

Emma pulled the books for her next class out of her locker, sighing.

Unfortunately, this was one of the classes that neither of her friends were in. It always seemed like time drug on and on in the classes where she was without Melissa or Kaylin.

She shoved the books in her backpack and slung it over her shoulder as she headed down the hall towards her next class. Halfway to her class, she heard a familiar voice behind her.

"Emma!"

Emma was already rolling her eyes as she turned around. Had she not made herself clear over the weekend?

"Luke, I'm still not interested in...," she began. But before she could finish her sentence, Luke had his hand firmly wrapped around hers and was pulling her into an empty room. He shut the door behind them, keeping the lights off.

Emma was so stunned that she didn't even have time to think about pulling away or protesting. So there she stood, inches from the face of one of her sworn enemies, eyes wide. Was he crazy?

Her heart pounded, although she couldn't understand why. She tried to control her breathing. What was wrong with her?

"Emma, hear me out, ok?" Luke pleaded quietly.

Well, it seemed he was going to go to any length to say whatever it was he had to say. Maybe she should just let him get it out so she could get out of here.

"Fine," she said shortly.

"I didn't mean to hit you that hard with the dodgeball, and I definitely didn't mean to hit you in the head," Luke said, his gaze was locked into hers.

Emma blinked, not sure what to say.

"Do you believe me?" Luke pressed.

Why did he care so much that she believed him? Or that it was an accident in the first place? Emma considered what his ulterior motive could be. And more importantly, did that ulterior motive involve Jaclyn and her friends?

"I don't know, Luke. Jaclyn hates me and has made it clear her life mission is to make me miserable, and her boyfriend is one of your best friends. Why *should* I believe you?" Emma asked.

Luke paused, considering her words. "I'm not like them," he said softly, his gaze dropping to the floor.

"For someone who isn't like those guys, you certainly seem to spend a lot of time with them!" Emma replied. She felt the heat creeping up her neck again. This was ridiculous. Why was she even wasting her time in a dark room alone with Luke anyway? He said what he needed to say, and that's all she had agreed to.

Luke opened his mouth to respond, but Emma held her hand up dismissively. "I have to get to class, the bell is probably about to ring any second."

Emma was reaching for the handle of the door when a loud, chirping alarm sounded. She paused, placing the sound. That wasn't the bell letting her know class had started. *That* was the lockdown drill alarm.

Emma spun around, her eyes locking onto Luke's expression which reflected her own surprise. "I didn't think we had a lockdown drill scheduled for today."

Luke shook his head. "We didn't."

Emma's head spun. That only meant one thing: this *wasn't* a drill. Her mind raced as she remembered all the possible reasons for a lockdown drill. Was someone roaming the halls with a gun? Or worse?

Emma locked the door to the room they were in and slid down the wall. Anyone looking in wouldn't be able to see her here. Luke sat down next to her, only inches away.

Great, now she was officially trapped in a dark room with Luke for who knows how long. If there really was some threat to the students roaming around the halls right now, this was the worst possible scenario. Emma fought the urge to go running down the hallway anyway to find another room to hide out in.

Emma leaned her head against the cold, concrete brick wall. Running away, from Luke and into danger, probably wasn't worth it.

Emma and Luke said nothing to one another for five long minutes. She felt Luke look her way once or twice and wondered what he was thinking about. She had to admit, it was a little scary knowing this was more than likely not a drill. No one even knew they were in here. Emma fought the small surge of panic that brought on.

"I'm sure we will be fine," Luke said, shooting her a warm smile.

Emma realized her facial expression had probably given her away. Shoot. The last thing she wanted to do was look weak in front of Luke Cromwell.

"I'm not worried," Emma lied.

"Ok," Luke replied, not sounding convinced.

More minutes ticked by slowly as they sat there silently. The more time went on, the more painful the silence became. The only other sound was the alarm chirping somewhere down the hallway.

Luke cleared his throat. "So, how was your ride this weekend?" he whispered. Was he really trying to make small talk? Honestly, at this point, Emma wasn't sure what was worse: the silence and her mind turning over what was going on outside that door or small talk with Luke. She supposed small talk with Luke was slightly less painful. At the very least, it was a temporary distraction.

"It was good," Emma said, half shrugging.

"That's nice," Luke replied.

Silence fell thick between them again. Well, it looked like she was going to have to ask Luke something too if she wanted the conversation to continue. Emma fought the urge to sigh audibly as she thought about what she could ask Luke.

Then it hit her. There *was* one thing she had wondered for some time. If she was going to be stuck in here with him, she may as well get the answer to this question at the very least.

"Why don't you ride anymore?" Emma asked, breaking the silence and turning towards him.

Luke's head whipped around, looking at her in surprise. He shifted, his gaze dropping to the ground.

Emma continued to stare him down until he spoke again. Why did such a simple question seem to make him so uncomfortable? Would he answer her this time or state it wasn't any of her business again?

"Um," Luke stammered, seeming to not know how to answer. "Why do you ask?"

"I just think it's strange your family owns a boarding barn and you don't ride anymore. I mean, you literally have a dozen horses your father owns. Riding horses is the most amazing feeling in the world. I work away most of my weekend while other girls are out at the mall shopping just so I can own *one* horse," Emma said, shaking her head. It still made no sense to her how someone could toss aside the opportunities Luke had.

Luke's cheeks flushed pink as his crystal blue eyes met Emma's. Emma was surprised by the vulnerability she saw in them. She had never noticed quite how blue they really were until now. They almost reminded her of the ocean. Maybe it was because she was avoiding eye contact with him at all times. Until now.

Luke hesitated, then finally spoke again. "It's mainly because of my dad. A few years ago, things changed between us and he started only paying attention to me when it involved training and winning at shows because it helped the farm's reputation. Dad lives and breathes the family horse business," Luke said shaking his head, blowing out a breath.

That was far from the answer Emma had expected. She figured it would be something to do with spending time with his dumb friends.

"So, what, you just quit riding altogether because your dad was so hard on you?" Emma asked, her tone a little softer this time.

Luke shrugged. "Pretty much."

"The whole dad thing aside...do you *miss* riding?" Emma asked.

"Sometimes I do. I never stopped liking the horses. I just lost the love of riding because it became all about competing to win," Luke replied.

"Why don't you just tell your dad you don't want to ride competitively anymore and just want to ride for fun?" Emma asked.

Luke made a chuckle-snort sound through his nose. "You don't know my dad the way I do. There's no such thing as riding for fun in his book."

Emma considered his words a moment. She rode because it was what she loved. It was her passion. Emma had looked through pages of barns in the phone book until she found a barn that had riding lesson rates that met her parents' budget. When she had been given Lexington, she knew it meant giving up a lot of her free time to do barn chores in exchange for board. But Luke had been born and raised into the horse world. Emma started riding and continued to do so because it was what she loved. Luke had started riding because, in a way, he didn't have a choice.

Emma was surprised by the tug of sympathy she felt towards Luke. It sounded like his dad was pretty hard on him.

"I'm sorry, Luke," Emma said, barely above a whisper.

"It's ok, I'm used to it," Luke replied, and a sad smile crossed his face before his gaze shifted to the floor again. Emma almost wished there was some way she could show Luke that riding didn't have to be all about training to compete. Luke may not be her friend, but the fact that horses had been ruined for anyone rubbed her the wrong way.

Luke's gaze met Emma's again and held it. Emma felt her heartbeat pick up a little. Emma remembered there was something else that she had wondered about Luke. His mother had not once been in the barn while Emma had been there. She hadn't even seen her outside their house across from the barn. Maybe his parents were separated or something and they kept it hidden? Luke was still looking at her. Maybe she should just ask about his mom too while they were still trapped here; she may never get another chance.

Emma opened her mouth to ask Luke why she had not once seen his mom in the three years she rode at his farm, but suddenly the hallway alarm stopped chirping.

Luke was already scrambling to get up, peeking out of the window of the class-room door.

"I think it's over," Luke said, his voice was a normal volume for the first time since the alarm started sounding. He slowly opened the classroom door and peeked out. With the door cracked, she could already hear the sound of students talking.

Luke looked over his shoulder one more time at Emma before heading out into the hallway without another word. Emma sat there an extra moment, processing.

Emma couldn't believe she was even thinking it, but she was beginning to wonder if there was more to Luke Cromwell than the cute, popular guy he came off as or the person she had sworn was no better than Jaclyn.

Now, with the information he had just shared, and the unanswered question still tugging at her mind, she was questioning everything she thought she knew about him.

ele

Emma walked beside Melissa and Kaylin as they headed to their final classes of the day.

"I still can't believe we were all locked in a dark, silent classroom for half an hour because some kid wanted to prank call a threat into the school," Melissa said, rolling her eyes. Melissa had made it clear when they first talked after the lockdown, that sitting silently for that long was something she'd prefer never to do again.

"I know! Who does that?" Kaylin agreed. "The worst part is that poor Emma wasn't even with us. At least we had each other," Kaylin said, looking over at Melissa.

"Seriously. What class were you stuck in again, Em?" Melissa asked.

Emma felt heat in her cheeks as she contemplated whether to tell her friends about being trapped in an empty classroom with Luke. After all, she hardly knew herself what to make of it.

"I was supposed to be in study hall, but...," Emma paused, chewing her lip. What would they think when she told them? And how much should she say? For some reason, it felt strange to tell even her closest friends about the part of the conversation where Luke had talked about his dad and why he stopped riding. Although she wasn't even sure why. Luke hadn't mentioned her *not* telling anyone. Still, the vulnerability in his eyes before he told her somehow felt like he was sharing a secret. Did his friends know about all of that?

"Of course they do, they're his friends," she thought. Still, maybe she should just leave that part out. At least for now.

"I actually ended up stuck in an empty classroom with Luke Cromwell."

Melissa stopped dead in her tracks, gasping aloud, her eyes wide. "No you didn't. That's awful! How did that even happen?"

The three of them now stood huddled along the wall of the hallway. Kaylin and Melissa leaned in, anxiously awaiting Emma's reply.

"I mean, it wasn't a big deal...," Emma began.

"Getting trapped for half an hour in a dark room with Luke Cromwell *is a* big deal. Wait, how did you end up in there with him in the first place?" Melissa asked.

"Well, he was trying to apologize for hitting me with the dodgeball. I wasn't having it at first, so he pulled me into the room and then right after that the lockdown alarm rang," Emma replied, shrugging, hoping Melissa wouldn't press for too many more details. She didn't want to lie to her friend, but she didn't know if she was comfortable airing out Luke's personal information.

"Rude! I'm sure it was completely miserable being locked in there with him, wasn't it?" Melissa pressed.

"It wasn't so bad," Emma replied, half shrugging.

"Emma, you were trapped with one of our sworn enemies. Of course it was miserable. You don't have to put on a brave face for us," Melissa said, resting a hand on Emma's shoulder. Emma chewed her lip again, feeling torn.

"Em, what aren't you telling me," Melissa said, her eyes narrowing. Melissa had been her best friend since middle school. Clearly, Emma wasn't doing a very good job at hiding her facial expressions.

"I mean yeah, it was *pretty* awful. We sat there in silence most of the time, and then he tried to make small talk," Emma replied.

Melissa held Emma's gaze a moment before turning to Kaylin. "Ugh, he would try to make small talk. Typical. Well, at least it's over now," Melissa said as she began walking back down the hall towards their class.

Emma blew out a silent breath, glad Melissa decided not to press her further. As much as she felt like she shouldn't go telling her friends about some of the more personal things Luke had shared, she still wasn't sure she would have lied to her friends to avoid it.

It was strange to her that only a couple hours ago she would have thrown Luke under the bus any chance she got. And now, for some reason, she felt the need to protect his privacy. Maybe that just meant she wasn't anything like Jaclyn, someone who would throw anyone under the bus the first moment she got.

Emma was sure things would go back to normal soon. Just because she knew some personal things about Luke didn't mean they were suddenly friends.

She just needed to remind herself of that.

Chapter Five

Emma sponged away the sweat from the saddle area on Lexington's back.

"We had a great ride, didn't we bud?" Emma cooed to the horse who was nuzzling her pockets for treats. Her lesson with Maggie had gone so well. Maggie had raised the jumps today to about two foot nine and Lexington had soared over them without hesitation. Really, Emma wasn't sure how she had been so lucky to get a horse like him.

"Your horse looked good today," a voice said, making Emma jump and turn around. She wasn't aware anyone else was still in the barn as Maggie had left right after their lesson.

Emma squinted, trying to make out the person leaning against the wooden barn door frame. She almost didn't recognize Luke with the setting sun's light shining behind him, making it hard to see. He had a boyish grin on his face. Pausing, Emma's mind raced. Normally she would tell Luke to bug off and find somewhere else to hold up a wall.

But today, she didn't feel the intense surge of anger that followed when Luke made his appearance at the barn, interrupting her time with her horse. Although she was still annoyed he was interrupting her sacred horse-time, she was surprised by her own reaction to Luke's appearance. Other than passing one another in the hallways, Emma had made no attempt to speak to Luke since the day they were trapped in the classroom, and neither had he. As predicted, he acted like she didn't exist once again.

"Where are all your annoying friends? Don't they usually accompany you when you decide to walk the barn aisles for no reason?" Emma asked, although her voice didn't have the same edge it normally did when she spoke to Luke. Was it because she now knew something about him that made her look at him just a little bit differently?

Emma reminded herself that Luke, and especially his buddies, were not to be trusted if she wanted to survive the rest of high school.

Luke laughed, and Emma thought it almost sounded genuine. "Nope, my friends are all at a game tonight," Luke replied.

"And you aren't with them?" Emma asked, although it came out as more of a statement. Still, she was genuinely curious. Luke and his buddies had proven to be all but inseparable, especially on a Friday night.

"Nah, not tonight. I decided to stay in," he added with a shrug.

That was definitely unusual. Oh well, she supposed even Luke needed a break from his gang of buddies now and then.

"How long were you watching my lesson? I didn't see you," Emma asked. Why had he even been watching in the first place? Just because he wasn't with his friends didn't mean he had nothing better to do than watch her ride her horse in circles.

"Just the last ten minutes or so. I needed to get out of the house, so I took a walk," Luke replied, but his gaze quickly dropped to the ground as he kicked at the dirt in the aisleway.

Emma saw the look on his face before it shifted to the ground. It was a similar look to when he had talked about his dad and why he stopped riding.

Before she could stop herself, the words were tumbling out. "Is everything ok?"

Luke met her gaze, his face reflecting the surprise of her question. It made sense she guessed, since anything else out of her mouth was usually telling him to get lost. He paused, like he wasn't sure he wanted to tell her.

"I needed a break from my dad," he said, taking a step closer to her. He was close to Lexington now, who reached out to sniff his pockets. Emma couldn't help but smile at the horse. He was always on the lookout for snacks. To her surprise, Luke pulled two horse cookies from his pocket and fed them to Lexington. Lexington crunched happily on the treats, cocking his hind leg.

"Why do you have horse treats?" Emma asked.

Luke half shrugged, "I like feeding treats to a few of my favorite horses," he replied.

Emma remembered him saying he still liked horses, despite the fact he didn't ride anymore. She had wondered how true that actually was. Now she realized he might just have been telling the truth.

"So, you needed a break from your dad?" Emma pressed. She couldn't help it; she wanted to know what could have forced Luke out of the house.

Luke eyed her, pausing again. Whatever it was, Luke didn't seem sure he could trust her with it.

"I didn't tell anyone about what you said the day of the lockdown," Emma blurted out. She decided to blame curiosity and wanting to know what drove him out here.

"Not even Melissa and Kaylin?" Luke asked, seeming surprised.

"No. I just said we small talked and left it at that," Emma said, adding a shrug to make sure he knew it wasn't a big deal.

Luke's eyes scrunched together a moment before he let out a sigh. "My dad gets a little bit on edge when he drinks too much. He doesn't do this all the time, but when he does...," Luke trailed off, looking away. He let out another sigh, then continued. "It doesn't take much for him to pick a fight when he gets like this. So I decided to take a walk before things got worse."

Emma suddenly felt bad for Luke. He seemed to be genuine about what he was saying. She reflexively took a step toward him, now only a few inches away from Luke. Emma tilted her head, studying his expression. Emma wondered what it was like to have a parent constantly be so hard on them. She was lucky both her parents had always been loving and so supportive of her in every way. It seemed Luke didn't have that in his life. But what about his mother?

"That must be really hard," she said, almost at a whisper. She hoped he understood she meant that. "What about your mom though? Is your relationship with her any better?"

Luke took a step back, and his expression shifted.

"My dad is probably wondering where I am. I had better go smooth things over," Luke said quickly. He gave Lexington a pat on the neck and then turned on his heels.

Just before he had reached the open barn entryway, he looked over his shoulder at Emma. "Thanks for not telling anyone," he said before walking into the setting sun.

Emma stood there, blinking.

Watching Luke walk away, a hundred questions raced through her mind. Luke had opened up to her about his dad for a second time. In a way, she almost felt like he trusted her. Which was strange enough considering they weren't friends. Although, the very definition of friendship involved trusting someone and sharing personal things. If Luke had done that twice now, what did that make them exactly?

Still, the moment she had finally asked about his mom he had shut down and walked away. Something was definitely strange there, and if Emma had to guess, it wasn't good.

Now more than ever she wondered what deep secret was being kept about Luke's mother. Her head swam as she unclipped Lexington and led him to his stall.

Luke had certainly surprised her tonight. Now, she was sure she wanted to know more about him and his family's secrets.

Emma decided not to tell Kaylin and Melissa about her conversation with Luke on Friday. After all, they wouldn't understand. She hardly understood it herself.

He seemed so appreciative that she hadn't told them before, and now that she knew even more about Luke, she didn't have the heart to betray him like that. At least, that's the conclusion she came to after thinking about it all weekend.

Emma had wondered if she would run into Luke at the barn while she was there Saturday and Sunday to feed the horses, but from what she could tell, he wasn't home the rest of the weekend. His truck was gone, so she guessed he had stayed at a friend's house or something. It made sense considering everything he told her Friday.

Emma felt oddly torn between keeping things from her friends and not outing Luke. If someone had told her a week ago she would be in this predicament, she would have laughed in their face.

But no matter how hard she tried to convince herself otherwise, Emma found herself thinking about Luke. She wondered where he was, how he was, and a million other questions about the secrets he still seemed to be keeping about his family.

The bell rang, pulling her from her thoughts and signaling this class of the day was over.

Emma shoved her books into her backpack and picked it up off the floor as she headed out of the classroom. She felt a wave of nerves as she considered running into Luke in the hallway today. Before, she was convinced that a handful of conversations wouldn't change how he acted around her at school. Now that he had opened up to her about his dad twice, Emma considered the possibility that he might just react outside of the norm.

Emma shook her head and the thoughts from her mind. What was wrong with her? She couldn't possibly be acting like the other girls at school who fawned all over Luke, gushing about how cute he was to their friends when they passed by him in the hallway. Still, this felt much different than those ogling, obsessed teenager girls. No, Emma and Luke had shared *real* conversations, and she was beginning to think he didn't even have them with his real friends. If she was truly honest with herself, she was beginning to view Luke as, dare she think it, *a friend*.

As she walked back to her locker at the end of the school day, Emma wondered if she was going to run into Luke at all. Of course, she always seemed to run into him when she didn't want to and now when she did, not once. It figured.

Melissa was talking non-stop about some show she was obsessed with. Emma nodded and smiled now and then, but instead of really listening to her friend, she found herself peering down every hallway as they walked.

"...and then he ended up kissing her out of nowhere! I'm telling you Emma, you have to watch this show," Melissa said, turning to face Emma, whose head was craned as she looked down another hallway.

"Em, what is with you today?" Melissa asked, putting her hands on her hips.

"Oh, sorry, er, yeah that sounds like a great show," Emma replied, purposely avoiding the question.

Melissa stared at her suspiciously a moment longer, then continued rambling about her movie date with her boyfriend that evening. Emma was glad Melissa didn't press her. She hated lying, especially to her best friend. But was simply omitting information lying? Emma wasn't sure. In fact there had never been anything she hadn't been able to tell Melissa and Kaylin. Until now.

The girls packed the books they needed for homework that evening and headed out the exterior school doors towards the parking lot. That's when Emma spotted Luke leaning against his truck, talking to one of his buddies. She felt her heartbeat pick up when she saw him. Although, she didn't know why. Maybe it had been the fact she had so many unanswered questions she had churned over the last few days.

"Emma? Did you hear me?" Melissa asked. Emma had not heard a word Melissa said. She was still staring at Luke.

Melissa's gaze followed Emma's.

"Oh gee, just look at him! Want me to go give him a piece of my mind? I mean first he hits you with a dodgeball, then he all but traps you in a room with him...," Melissa began, already taking a purposeful step towards Luke. Emma grabbed Melissa's arm, shooting her the most reassuring smile she could come up with.

"Melissa, really, I'm over it. It was no big deal, I promise," Emma said.

Melissa didn't look completely convinced. "Are you sure? Because it seems like maybe someone needs to put that cocky...," Melissa began, but was cut off by Emma's hand waving dismissively in the air. "Mel, really, he's not worth getting in trouble over," Emma said. For some reason, Emma felt bad for talking about Luke that way. Especially considering she had said way worse things about him in the past.

Melissa seemed to consider what Emma said and paused. "I guess you're right. He's lucky I want to get into a good college and don't need that on my record," Melissa said, her eyes rolling as she headed in the opposite direction now toward her car. Emma blew out her breath and followed behind her. Melissa gave Emma a hug before sliding into the driver's seat of her car.

Melissa rolled her window down. "I'll see you tomorrow!"

"See you!" Emma replied, waving back.

Emma looked over her shoulder and saw Luke's friend was now headed to his own car. Luke pushed himself off of the truck and opened the passenger side door, tossing his backpack into the seat.

Before Emma could reason with herself, she began walking towards Luke's truck. He looked up, meeting her gaze as she approached. A slight smile tugged at his lips and he offered a quick wave before shutting the passenger side door.

What was she doing? Emma had no idea what she was going to say to Luke once she reached him. It wasn't as if she was going to ask all the questions she had been thinking about right here in the school parking lot. Odds were, she was about to make a fool of herself. What if one of his other buddies came over? It wasn't as if they were *actually* friends. Would they ask what she was doing talking to him? Would he make some excuse up and pretend they were bickering, as usual?

Emma was a few feet from Luke now. She considered turning around and heading back to her own car without another word. But his eyes were still locked on hers and for some reason, that made it impossible to do anything but continue walking towards him.

"Hey Emma," Luke said, sounding surprised. Of course he was. *Her* approaching *him* was a first. In fact, she had spent most of high school running the opposite direction from him and his friends.

Emma felt her mouth go dry. What exactly was she supposed to say now? Hey, I just walked over here with absolutely nothing in particular to talk about?

"How was your weekend?" she managed to spit out.

"It was pretty good. I spent the night at Chad's on Saturday," Luke replied. He was still looking right at her, and she was having a hard time thinking straight.

"That's good," Emma replied.

"Well that was the world's most boring conversation," she thought.

Emma's mind turned over what she could say that was *less* boring than what she had said so far. Then, her mind locked on to something she had thought about over the weekend. It had rubbed her the wrong way when Luke had said he couldn't ride for fun. Emma had considered the fact that maybe he just needed the chance to know what riding without an agenda really felt like. That freedom horses gave her – Emma knew everyone should know what that felt like. Especially Luke.

"What are you doing this evening?" Emma asked quickly, before she talked herself out of it.

Luke tilted his head curiously. "Not much, why?"

"I have a surprise for you. Meet me at the barn at 7:30 pm?" she asked. Emma all but held her breath as she waited for his reply. Would he even want to meet with her? They had barely crossed the line from enemies to sort of friends, after all.

Luke's eyes widened slightly after she spoke. Clearly he hadn't expected that either. It was a far cry from her running him out of the barn any chance she got.

"Sure. See you at 7:30," Luke replied, and Emma noticed a slight smile cross his face briefly. He opened the door to his truck and climbed in, firing it up.

Emma turned on her heels and back to her car. Suddenly, she felt a wave of nerves flood her as she walked. Had she really just asked Luke, her once sworn enemy, to meet her at sunset? And when he found out what she had planned, how would he react?

Her head spun as she slid into the driver's seat of her new car. Well, ok, it was a very used Dodge Daytona with a few rust spots, but it was all hers thanks to the money she had been saving. She had been so consumed by wanting to talk to Luke she hadn't even showed it off to Melissa like she planned. And now, the first place she would be driving her car besides school would be to meet up with the one person she had sworn to hate for the rest of high school.

"What am I doing?" she thought for what felt like the hundredth time.

But it was too late now.

Emma officially had plans with Luke Cromwell this evening.

———— *ele* ————

Emma drove down the back road that led to the barn.

She had timed it perfectly. The sun was beginning to set, but there would still be that remnant of soft light for at least another thirty or forty minutes.

"Plenty of time," she thought.

Emma felt like butterflies were doing backflips in her stomach as her car's tires crunched against the gravel driveway. She scanned the part of the barn she could see as she pulled in. No Luke.

She checked the clock on her car's dashboard which read 7:29 pm.

"Maybe he isn't out here yet. Or, he's in the barn. Or worse, he decided not to come at all," she thought.

Had this been a stupid idea after all? Being stood up by Luke would be mortifying. Had he only agreed so he could stand her up and laugh about it with his friends instead?

Suddenly Emma was questioning everything she thought she now knew about Luke. It wasn't as if they had made a friendship pact, for heaven's sake. Emma fought the urge to turn the car around and save herself the embarrassment.

Then, movement on the far left side of the farm caught her eye. Luke was walking out of his back door in jeans and a hoodie. Emma let out a breath, suddenly feeling silly for overreacting. But the release of tension she felt knowing she wasn't stood up was quickly replaced with the surprise she had planned for Luke. A surprise she wasn't sure he would even like. What then?

"Too late for that now," she thought.

Emma parked her car on the far side of the barn so it wouldn't be visible to anyone who might be looking from inside the house.

Luke was standing a few feet away, leaning against the side of the barn's exterior as she got out of her car. "I wasn't sure if you would really come to be honest," Luke said in a teasing tone

Emma felt heat spread across her cheeks. "I wouldn't do that," Emma said softly.

Luke smiled warmly at her and stepped a few feet closer. "So, what is this surprise?" he asked.

The heat in her cheeks turned into an inferno. This was it. "Do me a favor? Keep an open mind," Emma asked, turning towards the barn's entrance before Luke had a chance to answer. She may as well rip off the band-aid and see how he was going to react to her little plan.

"Ok, I can do that I guess," Luke replied, suspicion heavy in his tone.

Emma walked into the tack room and pulled a bridle off the hook. She walked over and slid Lexington's stall door open, pulling him out. She slide the bit into his mouth and the bridle over his ears. Emma turned to face Luke, her own face still feeling hot, her heart racing. What was he going to say to *this*?

"Listen, I know you haven't ridden in a few years and that riding has not meant the same thing to you as it does for me. But I think maybe you just need a chance to see what it's like to ride without the pressure your dad put on you. So, I was thinking, there is only one way I know for sure to help you do that," Emma said. She paused a moment, waiting to see Luke's reply.

Luke's eyes widened as he looked from Emma to Lexington. "And what exactly did you have planned?" Luke asked, folding his arms over his chest.

Emma caught the hint of hesitation in his voice. He was putting the pieces together now for sure. "I know your dad never comes out to the barn after it starts getting dark, so he would never know. I want you to take Lexington out to the back pasture and ride him bareback. No saddle, no arena – just the feeling of the horse underneath you," Emma said, holding the reins out in Luke's direction.

Luke stood there with one eyebrow raised staring at her. She couldn't read his expression. Was he mad she had even suggested it?

"Emma, I don't know about this," Luke replied, his gaze shifting from her to Lexington and then back to her again.

"What do you have to lose?" Emma asked, barely above a whisper.

Emma took one more step forward and Lexington followed suit. He nudged Luke's chest, making him smile.

"See? Lexington loves to ride out on the fields. I promise, he won't let anything happen to you," Emma said.

Luke slowly uncrossed his arms and gingerly took the reins from Emma's hand. His skin lightly brushed against hers as he did. Emma met his eyes, only inches from hers now.

"I guess I *don't* have anything to lose, right?" he said, his voice low.

Emma was having a hard time finding words. "Right," she managed to finally say.

Luke led Lexington toward the mounting block. He softly patted the gelding's neck before swinging his leg over Lexington's back. Emma found herself beaming. Luke started laughing.

"What?" Emma asked.

"It's funny, I haven't been on the back of a horse in years but sitting here now," he paused, shaking his head, "it's like I never stopped riding."

Emma smiled warmly at him. She hoped there would never be a point in her life when she had to remember what riding felt like.

Luke clucked to Lexington as he headed toward the back pasture gate.

"Have fun!" Emma called out before Luke walked out of earshot.

Emma watched as Luke walked for several minutes. As each minute passed, she noticed he was becoming relaxed, moving with the horse's movement more naturally with each step. He was asking him to trot now and made almost a full lap of the pasture at that gait.

Emma sucked in a breath and held it as Luke asked her horse to canter. Lexington broke into his floaty canter obediently, and the smile that stretched across Luke's face told Emma one thing: he was feeling what she hoped he would. She leaned against the post next to her feeling proud of her meddling. Maybe now Luke would consider riding again. Or at the very least, sneaking out to take rides just like this when no one was watching.

Luke cantered laps around the pasture for a while. The sun's light was just starting to dissipate as he steered Lexington towards the pasture gate, stopping a few feet away from Emma. The smile still plastered on his face said it all.

"Have a good ride?" she asked, knowing the answer already.

Luke slid from Lexington's back and stepped closer to Emma. "Yes, thank you," he whispered, so close to her face she could almost feel his breath on her cheek.

Luke rested his hand gently on her shoulder, giving it a soft squeeze. Emma felt the butterflies doing backflips in her stomach again. It felt strange that her body reacted to his touch this way.

"You're welcome," she replied under her breath.

Her head spun. Was his face getting closer to hers? Maybe it was an optical illusion due to the poor lighting.

"Luke!" a man's voice yelled behind her. Emma jumped and turned around. Luke's father was standing a little way off, and he did not look happy.

"*What* are you doing?!" he yelled, anger dripping from each word.

"I...I'm...," Luke stammered, searching for words.

"Riding bareback? In the dark? What is wrong with you!" Luke's father scolded.

"It wasn't dark when I...," Luke began.

"Enough! Say goodbye and come home immediately," Luke's father said before turning around and all but stomping toward the house.

Emma saw the pained look on Luke's face. Almost as a reflex, she grabbed his hand. She felt the warmth of it, pausing in surprise at herself.

Luke shook his head and looked like he was on the verge of breaking down. He gently pulled his hand from hers and stepped away. "This was a bad idea, I should have never...," he trailed off.

"Never what? Remembered what it feels like to ride again?" Emma said defensively. Was he really denying what they both knew he felt while riding again? His face had said it all.

"I have to go," Luke said, passing her as he powerwalked towards his house.

"Luke!" Emma called after him. He ignored her and kept walking.

Emma watched him walk away until he disappeared with the sound of a slamming back door. Emma led Lexington back to his stall and took off his bridle.

"Good boy," she murmured, patting his neck before she slid the stall door shut.

Emma's mind raced as she walked back to her car. Her emotions felt jumbled and confused. One minute she was inches from Luke, sharing a moment that felt like they were in their own world. And the next...

Emma shook her head, clearing the image of Luke's dad from her mind. She had never seen that side of him before. Now, she understood why Luke had given up riding and why he seemed to have such a rough relationship with his father.

It was almost completely dark now as Emma slid into driver's seat of her car and started it up.

This certainly had *not* been how she expected the evening to play out.

Chapter Six

Emma hesitated before pulling open the front door to her high school.

After yesterday evening, she was dreading seeing Luke. The look on his face and the way he had pulled away from her was still etched into her mind. Everything had been going perfectly until Luke's father showed up.

Now, she wasn't sure if Luke would ever speak to her again. A few weeks ago, this would have been good news. But today, Emma found herself affected by that thought in a very different way.

Emma sighed audibly and let her backpack fall on the ground beside her. She mindlessly turned the dial on the lock attached to her locker. What would Luke say to her when she saw him today?

"Hey Em!" Melissa said, sliding next to Emma, leaning against a locker. "What did you write about for that essay Mr. Hartje assigned us yesterday? I had the hardest time thinking of what to write...," Melissa stopped talking the moment she saw Emma's wide-eyed deer-in-the-headlights look.

"You forgot, didn't you," Melissa added.

Emma nodded sheepishly. She had every intention of writing that essay after meeting up with Luke. But after how the night ended, she could think of nothing else, including that essay homework assignment.

"Don't worry, you still have a study hall before his class. Just get it done then!" Melissa said, giving Emma's arm a reassuring squeeze.

"Yeah, I'll just get it done in study hall," Emma replied halfheartedly, her gaze wandering to the other end of the hall where Luke's locker was located.

When Emma's gaze returned to Melissa, she knew she was busted. Melissa had her hands on her hips and was giving her a look. The kind that confirmed Melissa was on to her.

"Alright Emma, spill. Did you forget we've been friends since middle school? That means I know when something is off with you, and something is *definitely* off," Melissa said.

Emma's mind raced and she searched for how to reply to her best friend. It's not like she could hide the whole Luke thing forever – if there even was a Luke thing to hide anymore. At this point, she wasn't sure. It's not like they had been much of anything before last night as it was.

Emma let out a breath and scanned the hallway. There were students directly in earshot. "Not here," Emma replied under her breath.

Melissa made a waving motion and mouthed, "come here" to Kaylin whose locker was at the end of the row. Kaylin shoved a book in her locker and slammed it shut before powerwalking toward Emma and Melissa.

"Emma has a secret!" Melissa whispered when Kaylin was in earshot.

"Where can we go to talk? We only have ten minutes until first period," Emma asked. There was nowhere in the hallways someone wouldn't overhear them.

"Follow me," Melissa said, turning on her heels as she quickly headed down the hall. Melissa looked over her shoulder before opening a plain looking door without a window. Emma had never been through this door and had always wondered where it led.

The room was small, about half the size of a normal classroom. "What is this place?" Emma asked in a hushed tone as she scanned to room. It didn't feel like they were supposed to be in here.

"Don't worry, no one ever comes in here. Most of the school doesn't even know it exists anyway. This is what they call the green room; it's where I spent hours hanging out before the talent show last year. That door over there leads to the theatre stage," Melissa replied, pointing to it.

A couch and a small mini fridge were along the long wall, and a few costumes on racks were on the other side.

"Ok Em, we don't have much time. What is this big secret?" Kaylin asked.

"Yes, spill!" Melissa chimed in, leaning in closer.

Emma felt flushed. What were her friends going to think when she told them? She barely knew what to think about the whole situation herself. Perhaps talking it over with her best friends would be helpful after all?

"You guys probably won't even believe me when I tell you this, but, I sort of hung out with Luke," Emma said quickly, holding her breath as she waited for her friends' reactions.

Melissa gasped dramatically, clutching her chest. "Ok, you're right, I don't believe you. What do you mean you *hung out* with Luke?"

"Trust me, I didn't see this coming either," Emma replied feeling her cheeks grow hot.

"How did this even happen? I thought he was your sworn enemy, second only to Jaclyn Alcott!" Kaylin said, shaking her head in disbelief.

"Please tell me you're not going to cross over to the dark side and start hanging out with Luke, Jaclyn, and their other snobby friends," Melissa said.

Emma held her hand up in the air. "No, there is no way I would join their posse!" Emma said, chuckling a little.

"Ok, so, start from the beginning then. How did you go from hating Luke's guts to being, dare I say it, friends? If that's what you are?" Melissa asked, placing her hands on her hips.

"Well, I'm not sure exactly where it started. Technically I guess it started the day he offered me a ride to the barn after I missed the bus...,"

"Luke Cromwell offered *you* a ride?" Melissa chimed in, cutting Emma off.

"Shh, Mel! I want to hear the rest of this story before first period!" Kaylin hissed, turning to Melissa.

"Fine. Go on, Em," Melissa prompted.

"So anyway, he gave me a ride to the barn and we talked a little. Turns out, we have a few common interests. Crazy, I know. After that nothing changed, and we didn't speak. Until he nailed me in the face with a dodgeball, that is," Emma said.

"And then he pulled you into that empty classroom!" Melissa blurted out, her hand quickly covering her mouth. "Sorry!" Melissa apologized, cringing.

Emma laughed. "It's ok, and yes. He was trying to apologize to me in the hallway that day and I wasn't having it. Maybe he felt guilty? I don't know. So then he pulled me into the empty classroom across the hall and forced me to listen while he explained it was all an accident. I wasn't really interested in what he had to say, but the moment I tried to leave the classroom, the lockdown alarm started going off and we were trapped in there together. After a while, talking to Luke was somehow better than sitting there in the silence wondering what was going on in the hallway. I got to know some personal things about him. I've slowly been seeing there might be more to Luke than I originally thought," Emma said, shrugging.

"Wow," Kaylin said, her eyes wide.

"Ok, that makes sense I guess. But it still doesn't explain why you're acting weird today," Melissa pressed.

The heat in Emma's cheeks intensified. Being forced into conversation with Luke was one thing. Telling her friends she had asked him to hang out last night was another. Not to mention that if she told them everything that happened, she would also have to disclose the issues Luke had with his father. Could she trust her friends with that information? Would they spread those rumors around school like wildfire? Surely Luke would hate her and never speak to her again if that happened. Although, it seemed like that may the case anyway, given the circumstances of last night.

"I saw Luke last night. I asked him to meet me at the barn at sunset," Emma blurted out, causing both her friends to gasp in unison. The leaned in closer waiting for her to continue. "It wasn't quite like what you're thinking. In fact, it's the reason I haven't told either of you about becoming friends, or whatever we are, with Luke. Before I tell you about yesterday, I need you both to promise not to say anything to anyone. Promise?" Emma asked.

"Promise!" Melissa and Kaylin replied, eager to hear the answer.

Emma explained about Luke's dad and the rocky relationship they now had, and the reason he no longer rode horses. "I don't know what came over me, but I asked Luke to meet me so I could have him ride Lexington bareback and know what it felt like to ride horses without the pressure of his dad or training to win," Emma said.

"How did *that* go?" Kaylin asked.

"That part actually went great. After that though...," Emma began, chewing her lip. These were her best friends, so why did she feel like she was somehow betraying Luke by telling them?

"Whatever friendship you were forming is probably dead now anyway, and they already know a little about Luke and his father's relationship. So you may as well tell them," her inner voice reminded her.

Melissa and Kaylin were standing even closer now, hanging onto her every word.

"We were standing there after he rode, and he was thanking me...," Emma shook her head, remembering the strange connection she had felt between the two of them those few moments before they were interrupted. Had Luke felt it to? She cleared her throat before continuing.

"...but then his dad came out to the barn and was so mad. I've never seen that side of him before. Then it was like Luke was a different person. He pulled away from me, and the look on his face...," her voice broke, and she cleared her throat again.

"Wow Em, that's intense," Melissa said.

"Seriously," Kaylin chimed in.

The three girls turned their heads in unison towards the door as the bell rang.

"Crap, we're late. Ok Em, we will talk more later," Melissa said, giving her a quick hug before heading out the door with Kaylin on her heels.

"See you later, Emma!" Kaylin called over her shoulder as she stepped out of the green room.

Emma picked her backpack up off the floor. She headed towards the door slower than her friends had and pushed it open as she walked down the hallway towards her first class.

Emma wasn't sure if talking to her friends had been a good or a bad thing. In a way, she felt a weight has been lifted by telling them. But she also felt guilty about sharing something she had sworn to Luke she would keep to herself.

It was in that moment that Emma saw Luke, as if on cue, as he walked across an intersecting hallway quickly towards the classroom across the hall. Emma stopped dead in her tracks, staring directly at him.

Luke must have seen her standing there in the middle of the hallway out of the corner of his eye because he turned his head toward her. He paused for half a second and met her gaze. Emma felt her heart skip a beat then beat faster as she waited for him to say something. Anything.

But he didn't. A strange look crossed his face and he continued into the classroom without a word.

It shouldn't have bothered her. They were barely friendly, after all. But despite how she knew she *should* feel, that wasn't how she *actually* felt.

Emma felt a little bit like someone had just punched her in the gut.

A warm breeze blew through Emma's ponytail that stuck out from under her helmet as she cantered toward a small oxer.

"Three...two...one...," she counted down the strides in her head.

Lexington took a deep spot, tucking his legs up under him neatly as he cleared the fence. Emma turned her head as she searched for her next jump in the course Maggie had come up with during her lesson the other day.

Lexington lengthened his stride, taking the next jump, a vertical, at a long spot. Emma could feel the power of her horse under her as he pushed off his haunches. Emma cantered a twenty meter circle before asking her horse to walk.

"Good boy," Emma murmured as she ran her hand down his dark neck. Emma felt pleased with how Lexington had performed today, especially compared to her lesson. It had been the evening after she told her friends about what had happened with Luke, and with him completely blowing her off in the hallway that day, it was impossible to focus on her lesson. Luke had barely acknowledged her existence – just like how things were before they had become friends. Although Emma was beginning to think they actually hadn't ever been friends at all. He clearly wanted nothing to do with her now. She had been at the barn every evening since and he had not come out once. For all she knew, he was avoiding her on purpose.

The punched-in-her-gut feeling of that day had slowly been replaced by anger. It wasn't her fault his dad had busted them. She had done a nice thing by helping Luke see what riding without pressure could feel like. Clearly he had enjoyed himself, and then after one incident he had written her off just like that. Well, if he was going to be that flakey, then maybe they were never more than acquaintances in the first place. The guilt she felt about telling her friends about his secrets had also slowly drifted away with each passing day. Since they were clearly no longer friends, then what did it matter if they knew?

Emma slid from her now cooled off horse's back and gave him a quick kiss on his velvety soft nose. "You're the only man I need," she whispered to Lexington. His ears swiveled in her direction, making her smile.

"This is exactly why I should have stayed away from boys," Emma thought. She had let herself get caught up in that fleeting connection she had felt with Luke.

How had she let herself get to this point anyway? From now on, she was going to stay away from Luke Cromwell just like she should have done in the first place.

Emma looked up at the ticking clock above the teacher's desk.

It had been one of those days that felt like it would never end. It didn't help that it was Friday, either. Time likes to pass in lurches, and Emma found the last hour of a Friday afternoon always felt like the longest hour of the whole week. Especially this week.

When a week starts off the way hers had, with Luke going from an almost friend to someone she didn't make eye contact with in the hallway, it made it that much longer.

The moment the bell rang Emma jumped out of her seat and beelined for the classroom door. She barely heard the teacher say, "have a good weekend!" as she practically ran down the hall, dodging students walking and talking. Normally she met Melissa and Kaylin at their lockers at the end of the day, but today, Emma wanted nothing more than to leave school and not think about it for weekend.

Emma had packed the books she needed for this weekend's homework before last period, and now she headed straight to the back door of the school.

"I'll just call them tonight and apologize for not meeting them at the lockers," she thought. She was sure her friends would understand.

Emma pushed open the door that led to the student parking lot and closed her eyes half a second as she took in the warm spring air and sun hitting her face.

Finally, she was free of school and more importantly, Luke Cromwell. Emma couldn't take passing Luke in the hallway one more time, with him looking anywhere but at her. It made her blood boil. How could he pretend like they had never shared what they had? Emma reminded herself that perhaps it had all been one-sided. The connection she felt with Luke had only happened to her. Now, she just needed to take a few days to cleanse her palette of Luke and everything that reminded her of him.

Of course, that technically included the barn. Emma had decided to go even earlier in the morning to do her barn work and ride, long before Luke, his father, or anyone else was out there. She knew it wasn't a permanent solution, but it would buy her some time to not be quite so put off by seeing Luke for at least a few days.

At least, that was her plan.

Emma unlocked her car and tossed her backpack into her backseat.

"Emma!"

She turned around reflexively at the sound of her name, but her jaw dropped when she saw who was jogging full speed towards her car. Luke Cromwell.

"You've *got* to be kidding me!" she muttered under her breath. Emma turned back around and began opening her driver's side door. Whatever Luke had to say, she was less than interested in hearing it.

"Emma!" Luke called out again, and she could hear the sound of his sneakers on the pavement before shutting herself in the car. She started the car, hoping it would send a clear message about her lack of interest in having a conversation with him.

A knock on her window told her otherwise. Emma rolled her eyes before rolling down the window.

"What Luke," her words came out sharp. Maybe that would get her point across.

Luke paused, seeming a touch thrown off by her cold response. He put his hands on the car, leaning in a little. "Em, can we talk a minute?" he asked, noticing she had put the car in gear.

Emma was attempting to take her foot off the brake with him still latched onto her car.

"What, *now* you want to talk?" the words came out harsher this time.

Luke paused again, his face scrunching up. "I'm sorry....," he began. Emma held her hand up, stopping him from speaking.

"You know what Luke, whatever it is, I'm not interested in hearing it," Emma said, and she began rolling up her window. Luke jumped back right before she started pulling away.

Emma felt heat in her cheeks and her eyes burning as she drove off. All week she wished for nothing more than to tell Luke just how mad she was for how he was treating her. She had certainly made it clear to him how she felt just now. So why did she still feel bad?

Emma angrily wiped away a tear that slipped down her cheek. What was wrong with her? She got what she wanted and now she was crying about it? No, she had made her point. Luke would surely stay away from her now.

But somehow, that thought only made her feel worse.

Chapter Seven

Emma dumped grain into the feed tub of the last horse in the barn's aisle. Picking up the stack of grain buckets she had set down, Emma headed back up the aisle towards the hay shed. The sun had barely risen, and the barn was silent except for the sound of content horses happily munching their grain.

Emma smiled, enjoying the sound. It had become one of her favorite sounds in the world since she started feeding the horses on weekend mornings a few years ago.

Grabbing a wheelbarrow on her way, she filled it with a couple bales of hay at the shed before heading back to into the barn. She began tossing flakes of hay into each of the stalls. When Emma had reached the end of the aisle, she turned the wheelbarrow around and began heading back toward the hay shed again. It felt nice having the barn all to herself this morning.

That's when she saw Luke standing in the doorway of the barn staring at her.

Emma paused for half a second when she saw him before pushing the wheelbarrow forward again.

How long had he been there watching her? And why was he even out here? It was barely 7:00 am and Luke *never* came out to the barn this early on a Saturday. Not even close.

Emma sighed loudly, hoping he heard her, and avoided looking directly at him. The last time she stared directly into his crystal blue eyes it made her thoughts fuzzy. Emma marched past him purposely and headed towards the hay shed.

"Good morning," Luke said, his voice far too cheerful. Didn't he know what time it was? Or how mad she was at him for how he had acted all of last week? Emma was sure she had made her point yesterday when she all but rolled the car window up in his face.

Emma ignored his greeting and walked quickly towards the hay shed. Luke's footfalls could be heard behind her a little ways away. Still ignoring him, Emma stacked two more bales of hay on the wheelbarrow and pushed it directly past him as she headed towards the last aisle of the barn that needed hay.

"Come on, Emma, just hear me out," Luke pleaded, still following behind her as she walked back into the barn.

Emma continued to toss flakes of hay into horse stalls successfully without looking at Luke. But after she was finished, there was no avoiding him. He was still standing at the end of the aisle, the space between his eyes was scrunched up and he was looking directly at her. It was clear he wasn't going to leave her alone until he said whatever it was he wanted to say.

Emma set the wheelbarrow down with a thud and crossed her arms over her chest, resting her weight on one leg. She raised an eyebrow and allowed herself to look in Luke's direction but made a point to not look him directly in the eye.

"What is it, Luke?" she asked pointedly.

Luke took a few steps closer to Emma, now only a few feet away from her. His expression softened and Emma reminded herself not to be swayed by the remorseful look on his face.

"Look, I know I've been a jerk all week. I ignored you and that was unfair to you," Luke began, pausing and holding Emma's gaze. She felt him search her face for a response to his statement.

Emma held her ground and the annoyed look she hoped was still apparent on her face. No way he was going to treat her like that and think a simple apology would suffice.

After several seconds of thick silence, Luke continued. "It's just my dad...he really ripped me a new one that night. He got in my head and when I looked at you, it's all I could think about. I know it wasn't your fault, and what you did was actually really thoughtful," Luke said.

He stepped closer again, now only a foot away from Emma. He was looking directly into her eyes. Curiosity got the best of her, and she found her eyes locking onto his reflexively.

The strange fuzziness she felt the last time she stood this close to him returned. Why did he have that effect on her? He was even closer than the last time, and the scent of cologne lingering on his shirt drifted her way when the breeze blew through the aisleway.

Emma closed her eyes for a half a second to gather her thoughts. She remembered the anger written all over Luke's father's face and the pained look on Luke's when he walked away. It made sense, the way he responded to the situation, based on what she knew about Luke's father. Still, he had been wrong to treat her that way.

"You're right, you were a jerk," she replied, but her words didn't come out as harsh as she'd hoped. She dropped her gaze to the dirt on the ground.

"I know, and I'm so sorry," Luke said, barely above a whisper.

She met his gaze again and saw the sincerity of his words reflected in his blue eyes. Emma felt the anger she was trying to hold tight to slipping away.

Before she could answer, Luke stepped even closer to her, now merely inches from her. Emma gulped.

"Please forgive me?" Luke asked, his words were soft and pleading.

Emma stood there speechless, lost in his gaze as she tried to force her brain to process logic. His fingers brushed lightly against her skin, sending shivers up her arm.

"You have to promise not to do that again," Emma replied.

"I promise," Luke whispered back. He was so close now that she could feel his breath against her skin when he spoke. She wondered if he could hear her heart pounding in her chest.

Emma nodded, her throat had gone dry and she didn't trust her words anymore anyway. She was pretty sure the logic portion of her brain had completely stopped functioning.

"Friends then?" Luke suggested, a goofy, boyish half-grin stretching across his face.

"Ok," Emma managed to spit out, her gaze still locked into his.

"Good," Luke said, smiling widely now. He rested both hands on her shoulders and gave them a gentle squeeze before stepping back.

Emma felt a little dizzy as she watched Luke step away. It was like she and Luke had been in their own little world away from reality for a few minutes, and now she was coming back down from it.

"I'll see you later then?" Luke called over his shoulder as he headed out of the barn.

Emma simply nodded, still at a loss for words. She stared at him until he had rounded the corner and was out of sight. Leaning against the side of a stall door, she took a deep breath trying to ground herself.

Had she forgiven Luke, just like that? And more importantly, had she just made some sort of strange friendship pact with Luke? But the word friendship didn't seem quite right. The emotions and feelings that had washed over her as she was standing inches from Luke hadn't felt like friendship. It felt like something she had never experienced before.

Emma walked back over to the wheelbarrow still sitting in the middle of the barn aisle and pushed it back to the storage room.

"What just happened?" she thought, her mind racing.

The rest of the weekend passed for Emma in a blur of riding, homework, and thinking about what had occurred with Luke on Saturday morning. With her thoughts less jumbled now that he wasn't standing directly in front of her, she was able to process things logically.

Emma had come to one conclusion. She just needed to talk to Luke alone before she saw Melissa and Kaylin.

Emma arrived at school earlier than usual and parked in the student parking lot. But instead of going inside and waiting by her locker for her friends, she waited in the parking lot, leaning against her car.

"Come on Luke," she murmured to herself, checking her watch. If she waited much longer her friends would wonder where she was and would ask questions.

Emma fidgeted, waiting impatiently as she stared down the entrance to the student parking lot. Finally, she saw Luke's truck pulling in. Emma let out a breath and pushed herself off her car and jogged over to where he had parked.

Luke hopped out of the truck's driver's side, turning to Emma who was standing a few feet from the truck door. The corner of his lips twitched into a smile.

"I see you are taking this friendship thing seriously....," Luke began, but his words were cut off by Emma grabbing his arm and pulling him behind the truck. Luke's eyes widened as he met her gaze.

Emma looked around her to make sure no one was in earshot or able to see them. "We need to talk about that," she hissed.

"Why are we whispering?" Luke said at a normal volume.

"Shh!" Emma said, looking around again, hunching over. "Like I was saying, we need to talk about the whole friends thing," Emma replied.

"What about it?" Luke asked quieter this time, tilting his head curiously.

"Well, I was thinking about it over the weekend, and I think we should be more like secret friends," she said.

"*Secret* friends?" Luke repeated, chuckling a little.

"Yes, secret friends. Look, I barely managed to get off Jaclyn's hit list lately, and I would like to keep it that way. She would love nothing more than to make my high school existence miserable and seeing us together would give her all sorts of ammo. Not to mention, I'm still not entirely sure I can trust you not to flake out and decide not to talk to me for a week like last time," Emma said. She knew better this time than to let herself get lost in his eyes.

"I made you a promise; I'm not going to be a jerk like that again. Plus, I already took care of the Jaclyn situation," Luke said, a slight smirk crossed his face.

"What do you mean you *took care* of the Jaclyn situation?" Emma felt suddenly dizzy. What had Luke done?

"Well, after the whole dodgeball incident, I had a little talk with Jaclyn and told her she needed to back off, and that you had been through enough lately," Luke said, shrugging like it wasn't a big deal.

Emma groaned audibly and leaned against the back of the truck, resting the palm of her hand against her forehead. "You didn't...,"

"What? I thought you would be happy about this?" Luke replied, seeming confused.

Emma shook her head from side to side. "You don't understand. What you did is going to make things worse, not better. Trust me, I know Jaclyn; that only fueled her fire."

The space between Luke's eyes scrunched up in concern. "Gee, Em, I'm sorry, I had no idea. I was just trying to help," he said, leaning against the truck next to her. Emma met his gaze and saw the sincerity there. Her expression softened and she reflectively reached out and touched his arm.

"It's ok, I appreciate you trying to help," Emma replied.

"So, this secret friends thing. How does that work?" Luke asked.

Emma had considered the option of cutting ties with Luke and telling him being friends with him would be too difficult. After all, it's not as if they ran in the same circle of friends. Not even close. Plus, Jaclyn of all people would make her life miserable if she was friends with one of her boyfriend's best friends.

Still, the connection she felt with Luke made it impossible to execute that plan. And so, she had come up with her secret friends plan.

"Well, it's simple I guess. We can be friends, but we just can't tell any of our respective friends about it," Emma said, half shrugging.

"So, we just hang out in secret?" Luke asked.

"Basically," Emma replied.

Luke thought a moment then looked over at Emma and grinned. "Secret friend-ship pact?" he said, stretching out his hand toward her, offering for her to shake it.

Emma found herself smiling back as she put her hand in his, shaking it playfully. "Deal," she agreed.

Emma looked around, noticing how busy the parking lot had become. First period would be starting soon, and Luke's slew of annoying buddies would be pulling in at the last minute as usual. The other benefit of being secret friends with Luke was that she could continue to stay far away from them.

Emma picked up her backpack and turned back towards Luke.

"Meet me tomorrow after school in front of the barn? We may as well get started on this secret friendship stuff right away," Luke asked, a playful smile on his lips.

"Ok," Emma said, a smile tugging at her lips as she spoke.

"Have a good day," he replied, winking.

"Thanks, you too," Emma replied quickly before turning around and walking quickly towards the back door of the school.

Emma felt like a weight had been lifted. Maybe this plan of hers could work after all. All but jogging down the hallway towards her locker, she saw Kaylin and Melissa were leaning against it waiting for her.

"Em, where have you been?" Melissa asked as Emma quickly spun the dial locker.

"Sorry, just running late," she mumbled as she stuffed books back into her locker, exchanging them for the ones for her first few classes. Emma slammed her locker shut and picked up her bookbag.

"How was your weekend?" Kaylin asked as the three of them walked down the hall.

"Good, just went to the barn and worked on homework," Emma said with a shrug. Technically, that wasn't a lie.

"Sounds boring," Melissa replied, scrunching up her nose.

"Yeah...," Emma replied, her voice trailing off. Truth be told, it had been much less boring than Melissa assumed.

The secret friendship with Luke had seemed like such a good idea until seeing her friends this morning. As far as they knew, Luke was still ignoring her.

Emma just hoped she could juggle that secret without lying directly to her friends.

Emma stepped through the spongy spring grass towards the barn.

She felt her heart flutter when she saw Luke casually leaning against the side of the barn. His blue eyes lit up when she came into view and a slight smile crossed his face.

Emma took a deep breath and let her gaze fall to the ground in front of her as she tried to control her emotions. She still didn't quite understand why Luke had this effect on her.

It crossed her mind on the way here that while Luke had asked her to meet him after work, he had not mentioned what they would be doing.

"Hey there," Luke said in a low voice.

"Hey," Emma replied softly.

"I have a surprise for you," Luke said, his eyes twinkling with excitement.

Emma tilted her head curiously. "A surprise?"

"Yes, and one I'm sure you'll enjoy," Luke said, grinning widely now.

Without another word, Luke turned around and walked into the barn. Emma followed closely behind him, her curiosity piqued.

He made his way to the part of the aisle where the sets of cross-ties were located. There in the cross-ties was a fully-tacked up Lexington and Ducky, one of Luke's father's horses.

Emma gasped audibly, turning wide-eyed toward Luke. "What's *this*?"

"Tacked up horses, of course," Luke teased.

Emma rolled her eyes but smiled anyway. "Thank you captain obvious," Emma said, sarcasm dripping from her words. "I meant, what's this about? What about your dad?"

"Dad is out of town today visiting his niece who just had a baby. Plus, I figured I owed you a do-over from the last time you got me on a horse," Luke replied.

So it was just them on the farm today. Emma felt a strange feeling wash over her knowing that she and Luke were completely alone here. Of course, that wouldn't last long. Most of the boarders came out in the early evening to ride.

"Well, what are we waiting for then?" Emma beamed, taking the halter off her horse at the cross-ties and slipping the bridle over his head as she spoke. Luke smiled back and walked over to his horse, bridling him as well.

They walked the horses over to the mounting block and took turns swinging into the saddle. Emma looked over at Luke, almost in disbelief he was on a horse next to her. After years of never seeing him ride, it blew her mind a little that she had been the one to get him back in the saddle.

"Follow me, I have one more surprise for you," Luke said, looking over his shoulder as they walked along, a mischievous look on his face.

"What else could he possibly have to surprise me with?" Emma thought. The short list of possibilities ran through her mind, but nothing stood out.

Luke steered Ducky towards the outskirts of the pasture on the backside of the farm. They wound around the exterior of the fence perimeter until they reached the furthest part of the farm's property line.

Luke asked Ducky to halt and turned around in the saddle again.

"Ready?" he asked, the mischievous look flickering across his face again.

"Yes but...for what?"

"For a secret trail ride. I figured if we are going to be secret friends, we may as well go on a secret trail ride," he said, winking.

"Secret trail ride? But how? Your farm doesn't have any trails," Emma replied, looking around as if she had missed something for the last three years of riding here.

"No, you're right, my farm doesn't. But the neighbor's farm belongs to a close friend of my father's and they have a four-wheeler path back here," Luke said, his face lit up like he was proud of his secret path.

Emma's eyes widened. "How did I not know about this?"

"Well, technically no one else is allowed on it, but I don't count since the neighboring farm's owner is like an uncle to me. I've been coming back here since I was a kid. Sometimes I would take walks back here when I wanted to get away from the house...," Luke trailed off and dropped his gaze to the ground. Clearing his throat, he began speaking again. "Anyway, it's got miles of trails, and I thought maybe you'd enjoy riding back through there. You just have to promise to keep it a secret," Luke said, smiling again.

"I swear, I won't tell," Emma replied, her gaze drifting to the thick tree line in front of them. A secret trail in the woods? Boy, Luke sure did know his audience.

"We just need to head this way through the trees and it leads us to where we can connect with part of the trail," Luke said before clucking Ducky forward. Emma asked Lexington to walk forward as she followed Luke and Ducky into the forest.

Trees were covered in freshly popped buds, flowers, and small bright green leaves. Emma took in the quiet forest as the horses' hooves crunched against the leaves remaining from last fall. The smell of earth and warm spring air filled her lungs.

A few minutes later, Emma saw the wide dirt trail coming into view.

"Ready to go a little faster?" Luke asked.

"Always!" Emma replied.

Luke clucked to Ducky, who picked up a slow trot. Lexington began trotting when his friend did before she had a chance to ask, making Emma laugh. They continued down the trail at the trot awhile until Emma heard Luke ask Ducky to halt.

"I want to show you something," Luke said suddenly, turning Ducky away from the path and back into the thicker part of the forest.

Emma scanned the area, looking for what he might be referring to. Several moments later, a small fort made of thick tree branches and rope could be seen. It was built around a large tree with low hanging branches.

Luke halted Ducky in front of it and slid from his back. Emma dismounted Lexington and walked him over to Luke as her eyes swept over the homemade fort.

"I made this years ago with my dad. I come back here sometimes, just to see if it's still standing," Luke said, turning to face Emma.

Emma shook her head from side to side. "You built this? That's incredible," Emma replied.

The way it was constructed, she wouldn't have assumed a kid and his dad put it together.

"Yeah, I mean, my dad had the idea for the layout, but I spent half that summer looking for branches that would work and helping him put it together," Luke said, and Emma caught the look of pride in his eyes.

Emma wondered if Luke and his father had had a very different relationship years ago. She couldn't imagine Luke and his dad spending that much time together or building something like this now. What happened that had changed their relationship so much? Maybe it was simply the transition to being a teenager. Emma knew how her relationship with her parents had changed over the years. Still, it was nothing like what she had seen between Luke and his dad. But Luke's dad was clearly a sore subject, so she decided not to ask about it.

Luke ducked under the fort and sat down, still holding Ducky's reins in his hand. Emma sat beside him, holding Lexington's reins. Emma watched as Lexington cocked one leg, a sleepy look on his face.

"I'm glad you brought me out here," Emma said, looking around the forest. Birds chirped in a tree nearby and the wind blew through the leaves on the trees, but the forest was otherwise silent.

"I love it out here. I thought maybe you might too," Luke said, his gaze meeting hers. He held it, causing Emma to feel that same flutter in her chest that she had last time.

"I used to walk through the forest behind my parents' house every day in the summer when I was younger. Sometimes I still do when I'm not at the barn. I always felt a sense of magic when I was out there," Emma replied.

"That's how I feel out here too," Luke said. His eyes still held hers.

"You know, you're a lot different than when you're with your friends," Emma blurted out. Whoops, that probably came out wrong.

Luke laughed. "What do you mean?"

"I mean your friends are annoying, self-centered...," Emma began, biting her lip and trailing off halfway through her sentence. She probably shouldn't be talking quite so bluntly about his friends if she intended to stay one with Luke.

"Sorry, that came out a little harsh. What I mean is. I used to think you were *one* of them," she added.

Luke's gaze dropped to the ground. "I know, they can be a little...rude some-times," he replied. "Maybe I have been too in the past, and I'm sorry for that," Luke added.

"So why do you hang out with them then?" Emma asked. "No offense," she added quickly.

Luke chuckled a little, meeting her gaze again. "They are almost like family to me now. I've been friends with most of them since middle school, and lately, I sort of feel like if I stopped being friends with them, I wouldn't have anyone else," Luke replied. The space between his eyes was scrunched up a bit now.

Emma considered what he was saying. Clearly his dad wasn't someone he was close to, at least not anymore. His mom was who knows where, and that left just his friends. Emma recalled that he had stayed at Chad's the night he and his dad got in a fight after he caught him riding. His friends may have become jerks since they started high school, but it seemed like they were loyal to Luke and vice versa. Emma felt lucky for the friends she had that felt like sisters to her. Maybe Luke felt that way about his friends too, despite their very obvious flaws.

Emma gently set her hand on Luke's arm, looking into his eyes again. "I understand. It's just too bad they are real jerks to everyone else."

A slight smirk crossed her face. She pulled her hand from his arm and noticed the strange affect the warmth from his skin caused her.

"I'm sorry they can be like that sometimes," Luke replied, looking out into the forest.

They fell silent awhile, staring out into the thick woods in front of them.

"If you have friends you are that close with, why did you want to be friends with *me* anyway?" Emma asked. It was a question that had churned over in her mind since the day he had apologized and asked to be friends. Now, she was even more curious after Luke talked about his actual friends.

Luke turned to her with a slightly stunned look on his face. He paused, seeming to consider her question. His fingers lightly brushed against where hers rested on the ground, causing a tingling sensation to run up her arm. Her gaze flickered to his eyes reflexively.

"You're nothing like my other friends, but that's what I like about you," Luke said, barely above a whisper. "You're like no one I've ever met, actually. For some reason, I feel like I can tell you things I can't tell my other friends."

"Oh," Emma said breathlessly. She wasn't even sure how else to respond. It surprised her he felt that way about her.

"I guess what it boils down to is I can be myself around you," Luke said, shrugging.

"You can," Emma whispered back.

Luke didn't reply but held her gaze. Was it just her, or was he slowly getting closer? She could feel his breath on her skin now, confirming her suspicions. Emma barely breathed as Luke held her gaze only inches away. Her heart rate picked up, and she felt butterflies in her stomach.

The sound of a cracking branch made them both jump. Emma watched as a squirrel ran from one tree to another.

Luke smiled warmly, then gently shifted his weight away from her as he leaned against the back side of the fort. His gaze shifted back to the forest. Emma took a deep, silent breath. This secret friend thing was feeling surprisingly like a real date. Not that she had ever been on one, but still, she had to imagine this is how it might feel.

"Luke doesn't think of you like that," she reminded herself.

Why would he? Luke could probably date any girl in their class. Other girls had all but thrown themselves in his path, making their interests clear.

Still, Luke hardly dated despite the fact he had more than enough options. Emma had always assumed it was because he thought he was too good for most of the girls in her class. Now that she knew Luke the way she did, she wondered what the real reason was.

A pretty blonde named Katie had been his girlfriend for six months late last year, but their epic break-up in the middle of the hallway had been the end of that when it was publicly discovered she had kissed someone else. Since then, she had not seen Luke date anyone specifically.

If she had to guess, his dad probably was to blame for part of it. Asking him now about his dating life might make Luke think she was interested in dating him, which she wasn't, and ruin the friendship blossoming between them before it truly started. For some reason Luke trusted her, and Emma didn't want that to change.

"Ready to keep riding?" Luke asked as he stood up, brushing leaves and dirt off his legs.

"Sure," Emma said, being pulled from her thoughts. Luke reached his hand out, offering to help pull her from the ground.

"Thanks," Emma said with a shy smile when she was on her feet.

Emma found a log on the ground nearby to use as a makeshift mounting block to get on her tall gelding. Luke easily mounted back up on his much shorter horse and they headed down the four-wheeler path again.

Emma found her mind wandering as they headed deeper into the forest.

There was no way she could deny it now; she was beginning to care for Luke Cromwell despite her best efforts.

Emma almost forgot the class trip to the zoo was this week.

If Melissa hadn't called her last night reminding her to bring her permission slip, she would have been one of the sad few left behind while the rest of them enjoyed a class-free day.

Emma mentally reprimanded herself for being so careless. It wasn't like her to forget something like this. But her mind had been preoccupied lately.

"I'm so excited," Melissa said as she all but skipped beside Emma and Kaylin toward the buses that would be taking them to the zoo.

"Animals and no classes. What's not to like?" Kaylin agreed.

Emma couldn't help but feed off her friends' excitement. Perhaps this trip and some time with her friends would get her head out of the clouds. The last thing she wanted was to be one of those girls who thought about a guy all the time. Of course, she was still focused on riding and getting time in the saddle before the upcoming show where she and Lexington would be competing. It would be here before she knew it. But when she wasn't thinking about her horse, there seemed to be only one other person who was consistently slipping into her thoughts: Luke.

"Emma, come on!" Melissa called out, pulling her from her thoughts. She turned her head back towards the bus in front of her, and saw Melissa was halfway up the stairs of the bus and Emma hadn't seemed to notice she was next in line. Emma jogged up the stairs and slid into the seat next to her friend.

In a way, Emma wished she didn't know Luke was somewhere in the back of the bus. It made it that much harder not to want to turn around and see if she could catch a glimpse at him.

The trail ride she'd taken with Luke a few days ago had been on her mind all week. The more time she spent with Luke, the more she realized just how wrong she had been about him. What's more, Emma realized that she had begun to like the person Luke truly was. No one was more surprised than she was about that.

"Em, what do you think?" Melissa asked. Emma had been looking out the window lost in her own thoughts and only half listening to her friends' conversation.

Emma felt warmth in her cheeks. Once again, she hadn't been paying attention to the conversation. She really needed to not make a habit of this. "Um, about what? Sorry," Emma replied.

"Where we should go first when we get there. Safari animals or aquarium?" Kaylin prompted.

"Uh, Safari," Emma said, picking the first one that came to mind.

"That's two votes against your one Melissa, looks like it's safari first for the win," Kaylin said, beaming.

Melissa tossed a slight look of annoyance at Emma. "Dang, I thought for sure she would pick aquarium first."

Truth be told, that was Emma's favorite part of the zoo trip. "We're just saving the best for last," Emma said to Melissa, offering her a lighthearted smile.

"Fine," Melissa said, pouting a little.

The bus pulled up in front of the zoo entrance and the students exited quickly as they beelined for the front gates.

"Alright everyone, be sure to meet back here at 2:00 pm sharp!" the teacher called out.

"To safari land!" Kaylin said excitedly after checking the map.

Emma followed behind her friends and took in the zoo's familiar scenery. They made their way through each of the safari enclosures, stopping at their favorite animals along the way.

"Emma, I just realized you haven't said anything about the whole Luke situation lately," Melissa said, turning towards her as they walked along. Emma froze and tried to remind herself to act natural.

"What about it?" Emma replied.

"Well, is he still ignoring you?" Melissa asked. There it was, a point blank question she couldn't get around.

"He's um, I mean things are...," Emma trailed off, pretending to be interested in one of the animals in a nearby enclosure.

"Melissa, you know that's probably still a sore subject for her," Kaylin scolded Melissa, putting her hands on her hips.

"Sorry Em, I shouldn't have brought it up. You probably don't want to talk about it, do you?" Melissa asked.

Emma felt guilt rip through her. She knew this day would come. Her friends would eventually ask her about Luke, and she would have to lie to their faces about her secret friendship with him or break their pact and tell them everything, potentially ruining that friendship.

"I'd prefer we didn't talk about it," Emma replied, her gaze dropping to the ground.

"Totally understandable," Kaylin said, resting a hand on Emma's shoulder. Melissa looked a little bit like she still wanted to press Emma for details, but she didn't say anything else about it. Emma felt her body relax as time passed. Still, she knew this couldn't possibly be the last time her friends brought it up. What would she do then? Lie to her best friends?

They wound around the rest of the different themed areas of the zoo until there was only one left: the aquarium. The timing couldn't have been better. The rain that had been sprinkling down on and off the last few minutes had picked up.

"Finally!" Melissa said as they headed towards the aquarium building, which was now in sight. Kaylin and Emma jogged behind her, eager to get out of the rain.

Melissa reached the front door to the aquarium first and pushed it open with gusto. Emma watched as Melissa beelined to the nearest fish tank, pressing her face against the glass.

Emma took off her jacket and shook it free of raindrops. She ran her hand through her now wet hair, trying to squeeze out the excess water. The rain pounding on the roof above them continued to grow louder.

Looking over to her left where some stair step style seating was in front of the largest tank in the aquarium, Emma saw the one person she had hoped to avoid this trip: Jaclyn.

Emma grabbed Kaylin's hand, spinning her in Jaclyn's direction before dragging her to where Melissa's face was still pressed against the glass.

"Jaclyn sighting," Emma hissed, standing between Kaylin and Melissa. Melissa turned around and saw Jaclyn sitting with her boyfriend Chad and several of their friends. Emma couldn't help but wonder why Luke wasn't with them but noticed a few of his closest buddies were also missing.

"They must have branched off at some point," Emma thought.

"Ugh, why!" Melissa said, rolling her eyes.

Before Emma had a chance to say anything else, she saw the door across the room fly open, exposing the downpour outside. In ran Luke and several of his friends.

"Oh great, now *he's* here too," Melissa whispered.

Luke was laughing with his friends as they shook rain from their hair and wet clothes. Luke's friends were taking off their sweaters and jackets and shaking them out now, but Emma noticed Luke had only worn a t-shirt today. Luke pulled his shirt over his head, ringing out the soaking wet fabric.

Emma felt her jaw dropping reflexively. Her breath caught in her throat, and she snapped her jaw shut as she forced herself to peel her gaze away from Luke.

"It's like he's *trying* to show off how good looking he is," Melissa added, turning away from Luke and his friends to face Emma and Kaylin.

"Let's walk further into the aquarium. The last thing we need is Jaclyn and Luke ruining the rest of our day," Kaylin said, as she looped her arm threw Emma's and tossed her a sympathetic look.

Emma couldn't help herself. She briefly looked over her shoulder towards Luke and his friends. Luke was already staring after Emma and her friends, and she saw a slight smile tug at the corner of his lips when her eyes met his. Quickly turning around, Emma hoped no one else saw their brief eye contact.

They walked through the aquarium, stopping for a few minutes at each tank.

"Cool, the area where you can touch stingrays and stuff is next!" Melissa said excitedly. They entered a large room that had lots of smaller tanks scattered around. Some of the tanks stretched all the way up to the ceiling.

"I'm going to stand in line to touch a stingray. You guys coming?" Melissa asked.

"No, I don't really think I want to touch one. I'm just going to walk around and look at the other tanks," Kaylin replied, crinkling her nose.

"I'll hang back with Kaylin," Emma said.

"Ok, I'll come find you when I'm done," Melissa replied.

Kaylin and Emma headed to the far corner of the room as they looked in each of the tanks.

Kaylin turned to Emma. "I'm going to find to the restroom. I think we passed it somewhere on the way in here."

"I think so too. See you soon," Emma replied.

Kaylin headed out of the large room they were in and walked down the hallway they came from. Emma walked up to the next tank which had lots of striped and tropical looking fish in it. She had always had a pull towards the ocean, which is probably why she enjoyed the aquarium portion of the zoo so much. Emma watched as the fish swam in and out of the small coral reefs in their tank.

She all but jumped out of her skin and gasped audibly when she felt two hands on either side of her shoulders.

"Melissa you sca...," Emma began, but paused after she fully turned around.

"Luke?" she said breathlessly, grabbing his arm and pulling him quickly behind the fish tank so they wouldn't be seen.

"Got ya!" Luke said as he winked.

"Luke! Someone could have seen you!" Emma said, as she looked around anxiously. Even behind this tank they could still potentially be spotted.

Luke shrugged. "My friends are still way behind me. I told them I would be right back."

"Well mine aren't. Kaylin will be back any minute looking for me and Melissa is probably halfway finished touching stingrays," Emma said, her gaze shifting quickly to the entrance of the room where Kaylin would be coming from. A strand of still damp hair came loose from behind her ear and clung to her cheek as she moved.

"I just figured I would sneak away and say hi. I saw you were alone when I was walking through on my way to the gift shop to get something to drink," Luke replied casually.

Emma made the mistake of looking Luke in the eye. Hadn't she learned by now she couldn't trust herself to do so? Luke was holding her gaze now, making it hard to breath.

Luke's hand was suddenly inches from her, and his fingers grazed her skin as he brushed the lock of hair from her face, putting it back behind her ear.

"You had a hair...," he trailed off, like he didn't seem to have a good excuse for why he did it. As if he did it reflexively. Emma gulped. His touch had sent a shiver down her spine.

Emma was starting to realize how her feelings toward Luke had shifted. And that was entirely too dangerous. Maybe little things like what Luke had just done meant nothing to him, but they were starting to feel like *something* to her. The thing about this secret friends pact they never discussed, or that Emma hadn't originally considered, was just how in depth it was going to be. They had only officially hung out once, and already, Emma could see herself headed down a dangerous path. One that involved her feeling things for Luke he couldn't possibly feel for her.

Emma took one step back away from Luke hoping it would help her mind feel less fuzzy.

"Maybe we should take a little break from this secret friends thing," Emma said quickly before she talked herself out of it.

Luke's eyes widened slightly in surprise. "What do you mean? We just started hanging out...," he began.

"I know, but, I think maybe that wasn't the best idea," Emma's gaze dropped to the ground. "I don't like lying to my friends," she added quickly.

"I'm sorry, I don't want you to have to do that either," Luke said, looking concerned. "Maybe we should just take the secret part out and be just friends then?" Luke suggested. He stepped closer to her.

"No way, I told you why it has to stay a secret," Emma replied.

"Ok, so we stay secret friends then," Luke stated.

Emma opened her mouth ready to protest, but his close proximity was making it hard to think again. With his blue eyes locked onto hers she found herself mumbling, "ok," back to Luke instead.

That's when Emma saw Kaylin walking back from the restroom, scanning the room for Emma.

"Shoot, Kaylin's back, you have to go," Emma said, lightly pushing him towards the rear entrance of the room.

"See you later then," Luke said with a warm smile before he headed towards the door.

Emma turned on her heels as she walked towards Kaylin.

"I think Melissa's almost done," Kaylin said when Emma had reached her. She pointed to Melissa who was happily petting a stingray.

"Let's go see her," Emma replied, walking towards Melissa. Luke was still on his way out of the area and the last thing she wanted was to trigger another conversation if her friends spotted him.

"You guys seriously missed out," Melissa said, washing her hands at the wash station at the end of the petting area.

"I prefer to just look at the fish," Kaylin said, scrunching up her face when she glanced at the stingray tank.

"Ready to head to the next section?" Melissa asked.

"Sure," Kaylin replied.

They walked out of the room and Emma scanned the hallway ahead of them for Luke. Luckily, he was nowhere in sight.

"I need to tell you guys something," Melissa said, looking at her shoes.

Kaylin and Emma turned to look at Melissa who was biting her lip.

"What is it Mel?" Kaylin asked.

Melissa looked at Kaylin, then Emma. "Johnny broke up with me."

Kaylin let out an audible gasp before wrapping her arms around Melissa. "Why didn't you tell us earlier?"

Melissa shrugged. "I didn't want to ruin the whole day, so I figured I'd wait until the end."

Emma scowled, thinking about how Johnny had hurt her friend like this. This was exactly what she was afraid would happen. "Did he say why?"

"He said it felt like things were getting too serious, and he wanted to take a break," Melissa replied.

"You're kidding. That's the dumbest excuse for a break-up I've ever heard," Emma replied.

"If you need anything, you know we are here for you, right?" Kaylin asked.

"I know, thanks guys," Melissa replied with a weak smile.

Emma was seeing red now. How could Johnny hurt her best friend over such a stupid reason? If that's all it took to tear those two lovebirds apart, how much easier would it be for Luke to simply walk away from their secret friendship?

It was just one of the many reasons she needed to be cautious when trusting any boy. Including Luke Cromwell.

Chapter Eight

Emma walked through the halls of her school towards her locker.

Signs were already posted all over about the upcoming spring dance. A student was taping one up right next to Emma and Melissa's lockers when she reached it.

Melissa spun around with an excited look on her face after reading the flyer.

"We need to go dress shopping *this* weekend!" Melissa gushed.

"I can't believe it's already almost time for the spring dance," Emma replied, shaking her head from side to side.

"Well believe it, because it will be here before you know it and all the good dresses are going to be sold out," Melissa stated, placing her hands on her hips.

Emma laughed. "Ok, deal, we will go dress shopping this weekend."

Melissa seemed satisfied with that answer and shut her locker door.

"See you after class!" Melissa said, waving as she headed down the hallway.

Emma exchanged books at her locker and then headed down the opposite hallway. The butterflies danced around in her stomach as she rounded the corner knowing Luke's locker was on the other side. Emma expected his buddies to be with him but was pleasantly surprised when she saw Luke was alone.

Emma kept walking, forcing herself not to look over at Luke.

"It would be kind of obvious if I stopped and talked to him," she thought. It seemed like a good reason to not talk to Luke, anyway.

Since the field trip to the zoo a few days ago, Emma had purposely tried to avoid Luke. Until today, she had been successful. It wasn't that she didn't want to talk to Luke. In fact, it was precisely the reason she had been avoiding him. Emma knew she was starting to feel oddly drawn to him in a way she had never been drawn to anyone else. And it terrified her. She saw what heartbreak had done to other girls, including Melissa, and Emma didn't want that to happen to her.

Even so, she had come to the conclusion that she was apparently incapable of turning back now. It hadn't taken much for her to cave and agree to continue being secret friends with Luke. One look into those crystal blue eyes and she had been mouthing the words "ok" mindlessly.

Emma had hoped by avoiding Luke for a few days that perhaps she could come to her senses a little and maybe regain a little distance. If she was lucky, maybe she wouldn't feel some of the things she was feeling for Luke anymore.

But that theory went right out the window the moment Luke's gaze met hers in the hallway. Emma smiled shyly, tearing her gaze away before she did something stupid. Like talk to him in public.

"Hey," she heard Luke whisper as she began passing him. Emma paused, glancing around quickly to see if anyone they knew was close by.

"I'd better not...," she began in a hushed tone.

Luke held up a finger signaling her to wait as he pulled something from his locker. Emma shifted from one foot to the other as she waited nervously.

"I was going to find you and give this to you later, but since you're here," he whispered with a shrug. Luke discretely handed Emma a folded up note, smiled mischievously, and then returned to putting books in his locker.

Emma shoved the note into the back pocket of her jeans and walked away from Luke as quickly as she could manage.

Her head spun. So much for the few days of palette cleanse from Luke that she hoped would cure her of what she could only assume was a ridiculous crush.

"An unrequited crush," she reminded herself.

Luke felt that he could trust and open up to her because, let's face it, his friends were shallow and self-centered. It made sense why he had befriended her now. But that didn't mean it was anything more, and she just needed to remind herself of that.

Too bad the way her body reacted to his gaze or his touch was entirely different.

Emma blew out a breath as she continued down the hallway. The note was burning hole in her pocket. The bell rang, signaling her first class of the day was beginning. She slid into her seat seconds after it rang. The teacher in this period was the type that would take her note and read it to the entire class if he caught her with it.

That meant she had to wait until this class was over to read it, and Emma wasn't sure how on earth she was going to be able to wait that long to know what it said.

Emma fidgeted in her seat as she watched the clock on the wall.

"Thirty seconds," she thought. Thirty seconds until she could read what was inside the note Luke had passed her in the hallway. It had been the longest first period

of her life. What could he have possibly written? This was the first time he had done something like this.

"Don't get your hopes up," she reminded herself. Whatever was in that note was probably much less exciting than the endless possibilities she had churned over in her mind for the last hour.

The bell rang and Emma jumped to her feet. She was all but running down the hallway towards her locker. She could shield herself with the locker door so she could read it and...

"Emma! Perfect timing! Now I can walk you to our next class," Melissa said cheerfully, looping her arm through Emma's.

Emma quickly wiped the look of disappointment from her face. "Oh, yeah, good timing," Emma mumbled, forcing a smile.

Great, now she would have to wait even longer to read the note. There was no way she was going to be able to read it in front of Melissa without her wanting to know who it was from and read it too. Emma held back a sigh as they headed towards their next class.

She found herself glancing up at the clock far too often again. The note was still burning a hole in her pocket and once more, she was thinking about what it said. Then, she had a brilliant idea.

Emma stood and walked up to her teacher's desk. "Miss Anniston, may I please use the restroom?" Emma asked.

"Sure, but don't take too long though – we have some material that will be on next week's test that I will be going over soon," Miss Anniston said, handing her the hall pass.

"Of course," Emma said, although she was already heading toward the door. Powerwalking to the nearest women's room, Emma began pulling the note out of her pocket, ready to read it the moment she had locked herself in a stall. This time, she was going to read the note and there would be no one to interrupt her.

Or so she thought.

The moment Emma turned the corner towards the women's restroom, she saw Jaclyn was pushing the door open to the bathroom.

"Come on!" Emma groaned under her breath. She shoved the note back into her pocket.

Well, there was no way she was going into *that* bathroom. Turning on her heel, Emma began walking down the hallway towards her locker. She wasn't far from it at this point anyway. Maybe she could just stand there a moment and read it. The other set of restrooms was across the building.

Emma walked quickly and spun the combination on the locker's exterior when she reached it. Pulling the note quickly from her pocket, Emma began unfolding it. Her eyes quickly scanned the words on the wrinkled page.

E –

For our second official secret friends hangout, I thought we could meet at the Medallion Golf Course just after dark at 7:45 pm tomorrow for a night walk.

See you at hole six?

- Your secret friend

Emma felt her heart pounding as she reread the words, processing their meaning. A night walk on the golf course? It sounded like something straight out of a teen romance novel. Except, this wasn't a date.

Was it?

"Of course not," Emma reminded herself.

"What are you doing?" a voice behind her said, making her jump.

Jaclyn was standing in front of her with one eyebrow raised, her arms folded across her chest. Apparently whatever class she was in required her to pass

Emma's locker on her way back. Just her luck. Emma shoved the note into her back pocket reflexively.

"Um...," Emma stuttered, not sure how to respond.

"What was *that*," Jaclyn pressed. She was eyeing the pocket that Emma had shoved that note into.

So she *had* caught Emma reading it and then watched her hide it.

"A note from a friend," Emma managed to spit out as casually as she could manage. She added a shrug, hoping to appear nonchalant.

"I don't believe you," Jaclyn said, her eyes narrowing.

"Well, that's the truth," Emma replied. Technically, it was.

"Melissa and Kaylin are way too afraid of getting caught with notes in class to write or read them. So, who's the mystery boy?"

The downside of Jaclyn being a former friend is that she knew the three of them far too well.

"Who said it was a *boy*?" Emma replied, slamming her locker door.

Jaclyn made a snorting sound and rolled her eyes. "Please, you don't have any other friends. Process of elimination says it's some secret crush. Do your friends even know about him?" Jaclyn said. A slight smirk crossed her face.

Emma felt her face flush hot and red. She hoped Jaclyn couldn't see it knowing it would only give her away.

"I'll take that as a no," Jaclyn said, her gaze scanning Emma's now red face.

This was not good. If Jaclyn knew she had a secret crush, she would make it her mission to expose her. If Melissa and Kaylin found out from Jaclyn about Luke, they would no doubt feel betrayed and lied to. It even had the potential to ruin her friendship with them permanently.

Emma felt her jaw drop and slammed it shut.

"Ladies, what are we doing chatting in the hallway when you should be in class?" Mr. Crites, the school principle said, somewhere behind her. Emma didn't think her face could get any redder, but somehow it just had.

"Sorry," Emma mumbled, turning to face her principle.

"See you later," Jaclyn said, flipping her hair as she turned around to head back to class. Emma could see the devious look forming on her face before she did.

This was very, *very* bad.

Tree frogs and crickets sang in the distance as Emma trekked across the golf course towards hole number six. She was far from a golf expert, so she hoped she was in fact going in the right direction. A small wooden sign ahead told her she wasn't.

Emma doubled back, looking for another path that hopefully had another wood sign pointing her in the right direction. Luckily, the moon was full and so bright that she could actually see her own shadow as she walked. It was a crisp but comfortable sixty-three degrees. Perfect weather for a night walk.

"If I ever find hole six, that is," she thought.

A cloud of anxiety had hovered over her since yesterday afternoon. Jaclyn was on to her, and it would only be a matter of time before she figured out who Emma had secretly been spending time with. That was something Emma shouldn't risk. The simple answer was to break off the secret friendship with Luke now before they got caught.

But Emma had already tried that once, and it hadn't gone well. Hours before their scheduled meeting time today, she had toyed with the idea of not showing up at all. Standing up Luke without another word would surely send a clear message.

But as time ticked slowly by, that plan became harder to stick to. Emma found herself defenseless against the strong urge to meet up with Luke and see how the night would unfold. It was a somewhat random place to ask someone to meet. Why a golf course? Why hole six, in particular? Curiosity had her grabbing her car keys and heading to the golf course despite the list of reasons that should have kept her home.

So here she was, roaming around an empty golf course at night looking for the surprisingly hard to find hole six. There was a very good chance she would regret this decision, but right now, she didn't care.

Another small wooden sign with an arrow read holes 6 – 9 were down the path ahead.

"Finally!" she thought, picking up her pace now that she knew she was headed in the right direction.

As she approached, she could see Luke's shadowed figure leaning against a large oak tree next to the short green grass of the hole. Emma felt a smile tug at her lips as she approached him.

"You made it," Luke said, smiling when he saw her. Emma felt her heart racing in anticipation. She was here, and there was no going back now.

"I got lost. I didn't realize golf courses could be so confusing!" she admitted, blushing.

Luke let out a deep, genuine laugh. "First time wandering an empty golf course at night?"

"Golf courses in general aren't somewhere I frequent. Actually, I could probably count on one hand how many times I've been on a golf course," Emma replied.

"Well, you are in for a treat then," Luke said proudly.

"I take it *you* frequent golf courses at night then?" Emma asked. Had he brought other girls out here before?

Luke laughed again. "Not at night typically, just during the day. My dad has been a member of the golf course and country club since I was a kid. I know this course like the back of my hand at this point," Luke replied.

The golf course meet up was making a little more sense now.

"So can I ask...why hole six?" Emma asked, turning toward Luke. His face was dangerously easy to see no thanks to the full moon.

"This is where the course starts to get really scenic," he replied, his eyes twinkling. Emma found herself getting lost in them, standing there staring like an idiot. She finally caught herself, clearing her throat.

"So, uh, what's first on this adventure?" she stammered.

"Smooth," she thought.

"First, I'm taking you to the bridge," Luke replied, his face lighting up with excitement as he spoke.

A bridge? That did sound incredibly scenic – and romantic.

"Sounds good," Emma replied.

Luke led the way across the green until they reached the concrete path. Emma walked beside Luke and took in the gorgeous scenery of the golf course. Tall pines lined the path to one side, and Emma spotted several weeping willows as they approached the bridge. It was short and had an arched architecture to it. Emma imagined countless brides had taken wedding pictures there.

"Definitely romantic," she thought.

Emma found herself wondering what this little excursion would be like if Luke was more than just her friend. Would they kiss on the bridge under the moonlight? Walk hand in hand down the path? Emma pushed those thoughts from her mind the best she could as she stepped onto the wooden structure. This was *not* that kind of bridge walk.

A creek ran under the bridge and wound around an area with tall grass and trees. The sound of creatures hidden somewhere in the darkness was louder here, like they were singing them a song.

Emma hung her arms over the bridge's railing, staring down at the water babbling over the rocks below. The moonlight was reflecting off the current.

"This *is* pretty; you were right," Emma said breathlessly, taking in the scenery.

"I know. It's one of my favorite spots on the course," Luke replied, barely above a whisper. He stood next to Emma, hanging his arms over the railing too.

"One of? This isn't your favorite spot?" Emma asked curiously. She couldn't imagine a prettier location than right here.

"Nope. There is one other area of the golf course that trumps even this spot," Luke replied.

Emma turned to face Luke, scanning his expression. "Now *that* I can't wait to see," she replied. If it was better than *this* scenic location, it was sure to be stunning.

"I'll take you there next," he promised with a smile.

Emma's gaze returned to the water below. Her mind drifted, and soon she found herself worrying about Jaclyn and what she had seen again.

"There's something you should know," Emma said. Luke looked over at Emma and raised an eyebrow, waiting for her to continue.

"Jaclyn caught me reading your note. I don't think she saw what it said, but she guessed it was from some mystery boy. She thinks I have a secret crush...," Emma paused, realizing how it sounded. "Not that I have a crush on you. She just, um, thinks I have some secret boyfriend or something," Emma stammered, already feeling heat creep up her neck. This was coming out all wrong.

"So, Jaclyn thinks I'm your secret boyfriend?" Luke said, a slight smirk crossing his face.

"Well, she doesn't know it's *you* yet. But Jaclyn is not stupid, and it's only a matter of time before she catches us if we aren't careful. With being secret *friends*, I mean," Emma replied.

Luke glanced back out at the water, lacing his fingers together. "I guess we will have to be careful then," Luke replied, not looking up.

"I almost didn't come tonight because of it," Emma blurted out.

Luke spun around, reading her expression. "Emma Walker, you almost stood me up?" he asked in a teasing tone.

"No, I mean technically yes, but only because I can't have Jaclyn finding out. Like, ever. If my friends found out from Jaclyn about us being secret friends, or worse, if she claims we are secretly dating....," Emma trailed off shaking her head. "My friends would probably never forgive me for keeping this from them," she whispered.

"I see," Luke said quietly, returning his gaze to the water. Emma wondered what he was thinking. He stayed silent as they both watched the water running under the bridge below.

"Ready to go to the next location?" Luke asked a few minutes later.

"Yes," Emma replied.

Luke was quieter this time as they walked along. Had she really screwed things up by saying the words "secret crush?" Maybe he was rethinking the whole secret friendship thing because of it. Emma thought she made it clear that that was only what Jaclyn assumed, but what if he was reading more into it? The worst part was it was not far from the truth. Emma technically did have a secret crush on Luke. Not that she ever planned to tell him about it.

"Here it is," Luke said, motioning to the area off the path to their left. Emma looked over and saw a wide lake surrounded by trees and steep banks that could be seen at the opposite end of the water. It twinkled in the moonlight.

"Over here," Luke said as he walked towards the lake. A two-person sized wooden bench was set on the edge of the lake.

Luke sat down on the bench and motioned for Emma to sit beside him. Emma sat down and noticed the bench was small enough that sitting side by side without touching was impossible. Emma gulped and tried to keep herself distracted by looking out at the sparkling water and not thinking of the warmth coming off Luke sitting so close to her.

"This is an incredible view. I'm glad you brought me here," Emma said.

"A few years ago, I was going through kind of a rough time and would sometimes sit out here for hours while my dad golfed. Once, right after I got my driver's license, I found myself driving here and sat on this bench on a night just like this," Luke replied.

"Was that when things started getting strained between you and your dad?" Emma guessed.

Luke shifted uncomfortably on the bench beside her. He didn't reply at first, and Emma wondered if he was going to answer her at all. Maybe he didn't want to talk with her about his dad anymore.

"Can I tell you a secret?" Luke asked, turning completely around on the bench to face Emma. Emma turned around too, now face to face with Luke. Their eyes locked, and Emma watched as a pained expression crossed Luke's face.

"Of course," she whispered.

"My closest friends don't even know the details of what I'm about to tell you. Truth be told, I haven't really talked about it with anyone since it happened," Luke added, hesitating. Whatever he was about to say, Emma could tell it was big. Why was she the person he was telling this to? Did he really trust her that much? She reminded herself of the friends he had at school. Not exactly a tell-all-your-deep-dark-secrets-to bunch.

"Your secret is safe with me," Emma replied in a hushed tone.

Luke let out a slow breath before he spoke again. "The reason my dad and I have such a strained relationship...well, it has to do with my mom," Luke replied.

Emma felt her eyes widen reflexively and fought the urge to gasp. She had so many unanswered questions about his mother that she had been afraid to ask. Was he finally about to answer them all?

Luke's gaze dropped to the ground. "A few years ago, my mom left us. She left her phone, her rings, and her house key on the kitchen table. She didn't leave a note or anything, she just...vanished in the middle of the night," Luke said, his gaze returning to Emma's. The pained look was intensified now.

Without thinking, Emma placed her hand on top of Luke's on the bench. "Gee, Luke, I can't even imagine what that was like," Emma replied.

"It was hard, to say the least. Dad took it even harder. He started drinking more and became more reserved. He just seemed to get angrier at the world with each passing day," Luke said.

"And he started taking that anger out on you?" Emma guessed softly.

"Pretty much," Luke said.

"That wasn't fair to you. You were hurting too. For heaven's sake, you lost your mother overnight!" Emma said. Her blood was boiling thinking about how Luke's dad had treated him so unfairly. How could he take his anger about his wife leaving out on his own son? It wasn't his fault, after all.

"Yeah, I know. But what can I do, you know?" Luke said.

Emma felt Luke's fingers lightly slip through her own. Emma felt like her heart was going to beat right out of her chest. Could Luke hear it?

She told herself it meant nothing. He was hurting, and he was confessing his deepest, darkest secret. It was only natural for him to want to seek affection in this moment. Friends held hands sometimes anyway, right? His touch was sending a warm, tingling feeling up her arm that she was desperately trying to ignore.

"Thanks for listening," Luke said.

"I wish I could do more than listen," Emma admitted.

"Trust me, that's more than enough. All my friends know about my mom is that my parents are separated and that my mom moved out of state. Which is probably true, anyway," Luke said with a shrug.

"You really have no idea where she is? She hasn't tried to call or anything all these years later?" Emma asked tentatively. Why would a mother just disappear and never speak to her child again? It made no sense to her.

"No, not once," Luke replied.

The sadness in his eyes when he spoke was unmistakable. Emma couldn't imagine how a parent abandoning her without a word would feel. Poor Luke.

They held one another's gaze, fingers laced for what felt like a long time. But Emma knew it was probably only thirty seconds. Why did time seem to stand still when he looked into her eyes like this?

Emma felt that strange draw to Luke taking hold of her. She gently pulled her fingers from his and ran her hand through her hair, like it was an excuse for needing her hand back. His touch was doing odd things to her mind, and the longer she sat here, the worse she knew it would be for her when this secret friendship thing ended. And she was quite sure that at some point, Luke would surely be bored of her and move on.

Watching Melissa's broken heart had made a permanent impression on her: never, ever trust boys. Even Luke.

"I should probably head home; it's getting late," Emma said, forcing herself to look away from Luke. She stood up before she lost her nerve and lingered any longer.

"I'll walk you to your car," Luke replied, standing up too.

They walked side by side down the path towards the parking lot of the golf course.

Besides Luke's, her car was the only one in the lot. Emma pulled her car keys from her pocket, fiddling with them. She unlocked her driver's side door and pulled it open.

"Thanks again for listening tonight," Luke said. Emma turned around to face him, keeping one hand on the top of the car door for support. If anything, maybe it would keep her grounded into reality so she didn't do something stupid: like kiss Luke Cromwell.

"That would be incredibly stupid," she scolded herself.

Logically, it made no sense to waste her first kiss on a boy who didn't like her the same way, and he would surely run the other direction the moment she did. Maybe if she just kept reminding herself of that, she could keep herself in check. The heartbreak that would follow couldn't possibly be worth it. No matter what she felt for Luke.

"Anytime," Emma replied, trying to keep her gaze focused anywhere but his blue eyes. Luke took a step forward, and she could feel his gaze boring into hers. Her eyes flitted to his, making her dizzy. Was it just her imagination or was he leaning in? The lightheaded feeling was making spatial awareness impossible. No, he was definitely getting closer. Right?

His lips were a mere inches from hers.

"Definitely closer," she thought. Was her mind playing tricks on her? Was she only seeing what she wanted to see? Her heart raced, and she tried sucking in extra air through her nose to calm it.

"Goodnight Emma," Luke said. Before she could reply, she felt his arms wrap around her shoulders and he pulled her to his chest. Emma was suddenly enveloped in the scent coming off his jacket mixed with lingering cologne. She closed her eyes for half a second, taking in the feeling and the smell.

This was dangerous.

Emma pulled away using the last of her willpower and forced a brief smile. "Goodnight Luke," she said quickly, sliding into her car and shutting the door. Her mind slowly became clearer as she sat alone a couple moments, regrouping.

Emma started her car and began pulling away without looking at Luke.

"What was that?" her mind said over and over as she drove. Perhaps coming tonight had been a terrible mistake after all. But it was too late now.

The way she felt about Luke was irrevocable at this point.

ele

Emma buckled the strap under her helmet before swinging her leg into the saddle.

"Ok bud, this time, we got this," she said to her horse. Although, she meant it more to herself. After all, going off course at the last show had been her fault, not his.

Once again Jaclyn had entered her division. No coincidence, she was sure of that. A win somewhere like this would be bragging rights for the next year, and her odds of winning by dropping down a level went way up. But this time, Emma promised herself not to let Jaclyn Alcott get into her head no matter what.

This was her favorite show of all time. Mostly because the grounds of this show were beyond stunning and iconic. And why wouldn't they be? After all this was *the* Kentucky Horse Park. A place she had begged her parents to stop by any time they drove to Tennessee to visit her uncle.

Two years ago, Maggie had asked Emma and the other riders at the barn if they were interested in hauling down for the weekend-long show. Of course Emma had been interested. Why wouldn't she be when it was located at the most well-known show grounds in the mid-west? The only problem with this show was it was much more expensive than the local shows she typically attended.

So her parents made her a deal. She could attend every other year as long as she saved up half the money that it cost to haul down, stable, and rent a hotel for the two days they were there. While Emma wished she could show at this magical place every year, it simply wasn't in the cards for her.

Instead, she enjoyed every single second of it while it lasted.

Despite the fact that her mind had been heavily distracted by Luke Cromwell, especially since their night at the golf course a week ago, there was nothing that could have kept her from being prepared for this event. Even Luke.

Which is exactly why she had told Luke, via a very discreetly passed note in the hall on Monday, that she wouldn't be able to hang out at all this week. It had been a good excuse to get some needed distance anyway. This time, at least she had something even more powerful than her pull to Luke. And that was preparing for the biggest horse show she'd attend in two years.

Emma had gone to the barn and ridden every day after school this week. She had also added an extra lesson with Maggie, which meant doing additional work at the barn during the week to work off that lesson. In a way, it was a good thing she had been so busy. It made not thinking about Luke that much easier.

Her horse, and her riding, was the most important thing to her anyway. Maybe she just needed to keep her focus on it permanently and remove anything that got in her way of that. Which included Luke.

"Just take him on a nice, long walk, get him used to the sights and sounds of the grounds. This is a big atmosphere, and he has only been here once before. Let's ease him in before you show tomorrow, got it?" Maggie said, placing a hand on Emma's saddle.

"Got it," Emma told Maggie.

She clucked to Lexington and pointed him in the direction of the arenas she would be showing in. Emma beamed as they walked down the horse path towards the famous Rolex stadium. Horses were warming up or showing in every arena she passed. Golf carts whizzed by with trainers and riders who had been walking their courses.

"This is horse people heaven," she thought. She felt fortunate she was a mere three hour drive to a place as incredible as this. It was even more incredible to be walking her horse down the same paths where the professionals walked their horses before the Kentucky Three Day Event.

Lexington's ears swiveled as he took in the action around him. Emma gave him a pat, smiling down at him. He was taking everything in stride.

"Good boy," she murmured.

They had made it to the far side of the horse park now. Emma felt her jaw dropping as she took in the rolling hills of where they held the cross-country phase of the three-day event.

"Want to take a little spin around the field, bud?" Emma asked her horse, whose ears were pricked in its direction. Last time she had been here, she had been a little younger and much more nervous. Now, with a couple more years of riding experience, she was feeling fearless.

Gently asking for the trot, Lexington plodded into the open field eagerly. It felt like some sort of dream being out here. After reaching the more level part of the field, Emma made a kissing sound to her horse who broke into a soft but open canter.

Wind whistled past her ears as he cantered along. Emma was quite sure this was the best feeling in the entire world.

Chapter Nine

Emma felt butterflies doing backflips in her stomach as the entry gate to the ring she was showing in swung open. Emma bit her lip, trying to get her nerves under control.

Maggie looked over at her and patted her leg. "Being nervous just means you are passionate about what you're doing. It means you want to do well. But remember, you can't let those nerves take over and keep you from riding. You need to turn those nerves back into passion – got it?" Maggie said encouragingly.

Emma nodded. Maggie had told her something like that at her very first horse show. She remembered thinking about it right before going on course and ended up getting second place that day.

"I'll remember," Emma promised.

"Good. Trust your horse, and have fun, ok?" Maggie replied.

"Got it," Emma said, with more determination this time. She walked towards the entry gate, shortening her reins.

Emma knew Jaclyn was probably somewhere on the sidelines watching her and hoping to mess with her head like last time. But this was Kentucky, and unlike Jaclyn, this kind of showing opportunity didn't happen often for her.

With Maggie's voice in her head, she locked on to that determination and passion and promised herself to not let anything, or anyone, get in the way of riding the best round she could.

"Next in the ring is number two-hundred and seventy, Lexington ridden by Emma Walker," the announcer's voice said as it echoed across the ring. A tiny wave of nerves threated to bubble up when she heard her name on the loud speaker.

Emma gave her horse a quick pat before asking him to canter. Halfway through her courtesy circle, she saw Jaclyn mounted up on her horse with Chad standing beside them. But what she hadn't expected to see was Luke standing next to Chad. Emma quickly peeled her eyes from them and focused on the arena in front of her.

Emma had worked extra hard to save up the money to enter both the hunter and jumper classes this weekend, and there was no way she was going to let herself be distracted. Even by Luke.

She could wonder why he was here later. Right now, she needed to focus on the first fence of this hunter round. A natural birch looking fence dressed up with flower boxes was only a few strides away.

"Three...two...one...," she counted in her head before Lexington left the ground and floated gracefully over the jump. Emma felt a smile tug at her lips. Her hard work seemed like it was paying off. His ears were pricked forward as she pointed him towards the outside line. He took a slightly long spot to the vertical, and Emma sat up as she brought him back a little after the fence to make up the striding.

"Two...one...," she counted again, and Lexington took the last fence in the line at a perfect distance.

Emma sang a song in her head, a trick Maggie taught her for keeping a steady rhythm on course.

"If the song speeds up or slows down, you know your course rhythm is off too," Maggie had said.

She legged Lexington up as they approached the final line. He floated over fence one with ease, and Emma continued to leg him on to get the distance to the final fence. As she landed, a wide grin formed on her face. That had been an exceptional round, she was sure of it.

The look on Maggie's face told her she agreed. "Emma that was lovely! Don't be surprised if you place well," Maggie said.

"Thank you," Emma replied, still beaming.

"Walk him out well and then be sure to cold hose him. I'll see you back at the barn in a bit," Maggie said.

Emma steered Lexington towards the back side of the horse park, where green, rolling hills stretched further than her eye could see.

"My good boy," she murmured to her horse, running her hands down his neck.

But as Emma circled back to the show stables, she saw a familiar figure standing on the edge of the field. Emma turned her horse towards Luke and walked over to him quickly.

"Luke, *what* are you doing here?" Emma asked quickly when she reached him. And more importantly, where was Jaclyn? Emma quickly scanned the area for her. Surely Luke wouldn't be standing there watching her ride if Jaclyn was nearby. Still, it seemed entirely too risky.

"Chad invited me along. He's here to watch Jaclyn," Luke replied.

Well, that did make sense. He and Chad were practically attached at the hip, and so were Chad and Jaclyn.

"Where's Jaclyn?" Emma asked.

"She's walking her horse out too, but she's on the other side of the park. Chad is with her," Luke replied.

"And where do they think *you* are?" Emma asked. Surely it would seem suspicious of Luke to walk off from his friends randomly, especially here at a horse event. Jaclyn was already on high alert waiting to catch Emma and her mystery crush.

"I told them I was going to go find some food," Luke said with a shrug. Well, at least that seemed like a plausible reason for him to be gone.

Emma felt herself relax a little. Perhaps she was overreacting. After all, Jaclyn was across the park. Now that she was done showing, which was the reason she told Luke she couldn't hang out, there was no excuse not to see him after she returned home. Or even right now, for that matter.

"How did you feel about your round? It looked great from the sidelines," Luke said. Emma had to admit, Luke understanding horse showing was nice. It was the kind of thing that would make dating Luke that much easier. Too bad *that* was never going to happen.

"It felt amazing. Lex and I brought our A game today," Emma said smiling, looking down to pat Lexington's neck.

"Luke, there you are," a voice said. Emma's head flung up, eyes wide in recognition of the voice.

"Emma?" Jaclyn said, sounding surprised when she saw who Luke was talking to. Emma felt her heart begin to beat faster. This was it. They were officially busted. A thousand outcomes began racing through her mind.

"I got lost looking for food and ran into Emma," Luke said. He sounded much more casual than she would have if she had attempted to speak. Forming words right now probably wouldn't have been possible anyway.

Jaclyn looked at Luke, then Emma. Emma scanned Jaclyn's face for some indication that she was putting the pieces together. Had she heard them talking?

"Don't you two, like, hate each other?" Jaclyn replied, suspicion creeping into her tone.

Emma gulped. "Yeah, um, I have to get Lex cold hosed anyway," Emma replied quickly. She was already asking her horse to move forward as she spoke. She needed to get away from Jaclyn's prying eyes before something on her face gave everything away.

"See you later, Emma," Luke called after her. Emma grimaced, thankful Jaclyn couldn't see her face now. Emma didn't reply, for fear of sounding overly friendly. See you later? Ugh, that wasn't what someone said to someone they despised when they walked away. Which as far as Jaclyn knew, was still the case with her and Luke.

Things were starting to get way too complicated. Emma felt like she was on the verge of her sworn enemy finding out about them.

It seemed like it was only a matter of time.

It seemed like discretely passing notes was their only safe form of in-school communication now. Although *safe* was a loose term.

With Jaclyn's watchful eye waiting for Emma to slip up and expose her secret crush, she couldn't be too careful. Every note she and Luke exchanged felt like a lucky break. It was as if she was just waiting for a poorly-timed hand-off that would lead to Jaclyn busting them once and for all. Emma found herself once again wondering when things became so complicated?

Even Emma had been surprised that Jaclyn hadn't put two and two together when she caught Emma and Luke talking at the horse show. In his most recent note, he promised Jaclyn had bought the whole, "I ran into Emma and politely told her, good ride," line that Luke fed her. He claimed he used the excuse that she rode at his father's barn, and that it would be in poor business taste to have simply ignored Emma.

Emma felt only slightly comforted by this, knowing that if Jaclyn caught them exchanging a conversation even once more that she would surely put the pieces together.

Still, Emma was powerless to end this secret friendship deal with Luke. She wished she could simply walk away, forever guaranteeing it stay secret. But her feelings for Luke had only grown since the night at the golf course when he had opened up about his mother.

Emma pulled Luke's most recent note from her pocket and leaned as deeply into her locker as she could to read it discretely.

E –

Glad you placed third in your hunter round over the weekend.

Can we meet after school today? Meet me on foot at the secret trail head behind the farm. I have something important to tell you.

- Your secret friend

Emma felt her heart race as she crumpled the piece of paper up before tossing it into the bottom of her backpack. She ripped a small piece of paper off the notepad she now kept handy on the top shelf of her locker.

L –

I'll be there.

- Your secret friend

Emma folded the note into a tiny square and put it in her pocket. She would hand it off to Luke whenever she could find a safe time to do so. Her mind drifted to the last line of his note. What was this important thing he wanted to tell her?

"What if he wants to tell you in person the secret friends thing is off?" she thought.

After all, things had been getting worse when it came to keeping it an actual secret. Or maybe he wanted to stop hiding? No, Emma had made it clear that wasn't an option. At this point, her only guess was that Luke was having second thoughts about keeping up this charade.

"Ready for gym?" Melissa's voice made her jump.

"Whoa, sorry, didn't mean to scare you," Melissa said, eyeing her suspiciously.

"Yes, um, sorry," Emma stammered.

"Have you had your dress altered yet? I know it was a little long when you tried it on at the store. You don't want it to trip you up on the dance floor, you know," Melissa said.

"Don't worry, it's being altered this week. It will be ready on time, I promise," Emma said, smiling over at Melissa.

"Good, because we need to look stunning. It can't hurt to make Johnny realize what he broke up with," Melissa said. A sad, but determined look crossed her face.

Emma stopped walking and turned to face Melissa, placing both hands on either side of her cheeks.

"Listen, Johnny is an idiot for breaking up with you, don't forget that. I'm sure he will realize what a stupid thing breaking up with you was at the dance, because you will look radiant," Emma said, shooting Melissa a reassuring look.

"Thanks, Em," Melissa said quietly.

"Come on, let's go see if we can ace some volleyballs at Jaclyn and her friends' heads," Emma said with a mischievous look.

"Too bad Johnny isn't in our gym class. I suppose I could just pretend Jaclyn is Johnny. I know that would make us *both* feel better," Melissa replied playfully.

After they changed into their gym clothes, they headed into the gym where most of the students had already gathered.

"I'm going to grab us a couple volleyballs so we can warm up our power hitting hands," Emma said to Melissa.

Emma headed to the rack where the volleyballs were stacked. She tossed a quick look over to Luke, who briefly met her gaze before she looked away. It was funny how good they were getting at finding discrete ways to pass notes. One look and the other knew what it meant, and the look she had just given him signaled it was time for a hand off.

Emma walked slower, knowing Luke was headed this way from across the gym. Emma casually pretended to be checking the volleyballs for air.

"Hey," Luke whispered under his breath when he reached her. Emma smiled briefly at Luke, meeting his gaze for half a second as she pulled the note from her gym shorts pocket and slid it under a volleyball. Luke picked up the volleyball and the note simultaneously, and Emma turned around and headed back toward Melissa.

"Ready to rock volleyball week?" she asked her friend, launching the ball off her fingertips.

"Ready!" Melissa said, bumping the ball back to Emma.

But Emma's mind was already wandering as she thought about meeting with Luke after school. And more specifically, to find out what this mysterious important question was.

Emma headed to the back side of the farm towards the spot Luke had showed her the first time he had taken her down this trail. She felt a buzz of emotions as she drew closer. Luke was leaning against a tree with his hands in his pockets waiting for her. She tried reading the expression on his face. Was he happy? Sad? What was this important thing he planned to tell her in such a discrete location?

"Hey there," Emma said as casually as she could manage when she reached Luke. A brief, worried crease formed between his eyes, but then he smiled warmly at her.

"Hey, I'm glad you could make it," Luke replied softly.

"Of course. So you had something you wanted to tell me?" Emma asked. May as well rip off the band-aid and see what this was all about. If it was the end of the secret friendship, she wasn't interested in dragging it out.

Luke glanced around quickly, looking almost nervous. "Let's take a walk," he replied.

Emma felt her heart beating faster. Something about the way Luke was acting made her nervous. If he was ending things, why did he need to take her deep into the woods to do it? And why did he seem nervous about anyone seeing them go back there? None of it was adding up.

"Is everything ok?" Emma finally asked after they had walked along silently for a few minutes. Luke's normally carefree demeaner was replaced with one that she didn't recognize. His body looked stiff as he walked, and that crease was forming between his eyes again.

Luke tossed her a concerned look. "I'll tell you once we get to the fort," he replied.

Emma nodded and offered him a weak smile in reply. Why did he want to get to the fort before they talked? Emma felt nerves bubbling up. Something *definitely* wasn't right.

Luke didn't say anything else to her until they reached the fort. He crawled in and sat down on the dirt floor. Emma sat across from him, a concerned look forming on her face.

"Ok Luke, I'm officially worried. What's going on?"

Luke did a quick scan of the woods. When he seemed satisfied they were truly alone, he pulled an envelope from his pocket. Emma's eyes widened. That wasn't what she had expected.

When Luke's blue eyes met Emma's the concern in them was apparent. "It's from my mom," Luke said in a hushed tone.

"What?" Emma blurted out, probably too loudly. Shock was surely written all over her face. What didn't make sense was Luke's reaction to this letter. Why did he seem so put-off by it? Shouldn't he be happy his mother had finally reached out?

"I found it in the mailbox last night. It doesn't have a return address, just the stamp from the city it came from, but it was addressed to just me. I had no idea who it was from until I opened it," Luke replied. He pulled the top part of the envelope open and pulled out the folded letter.

He turned it around, showing Emma the front side of it which had a few handwritten words on it.

"Read this alone," it said.

Emma shook her head, not sure what to say. "What does the letter say?" Emma asked. Curiosity was burning in her brain. After years of silence his mother had finally written him. Why? And what could she have possibly said that had Luke so nervous?

Luke held out the letter to Emma who took it gingerly. "You have to promise this stays between us?" he said.

"I promise," she whispered back. Emma's eyes began scanning the words on the creased letter.

My dearest Luke,

I'm sure this letter will come as quite a shock after so many years of silence from me. I'm sorry for that. I'm sorry for a lot of things, like the way I had to leave you without any explanation. I can imagine the hurt and confusion that caused you.

I wish I could say I would do it all differently if given the chance, but I can't. I had a reason for leaving the way I did. It's the same reason I left you and your father in the first place: to keep you safe.

I know none of this will make sense, and I wish I could explain it all to you. But keeping you and your father safe is my top priority. And at least for now, the only way I can do that is to stay far away from you both.

Maybe there will come a day when it doesn't have to be like this, but for now, know I will always love you.

Be brave and know that while I can't be there with you, I am always thinking of you.

Love,

Mom

P.S. Do not show this letter to anyone, even your father. Burn this letter after reading it. Remember, it's for your own safety.

Emma felt her jaw dropping as she read the letter a second time. So many questions ran through her mind. She imagined they were the same questions that Luke had when he first read his mother's words.

She gently folded the letter and handed it back to Luke. As soon as he had the letter back in his hands, he stood up and walked purposefully over towards an area that had no trees nearby and started to clear the brush away. It appeared that Luke was going to burn the letter like his mother had instructed, right then. The look on his face had Emma standing up too, and she began clearing away leaves with him as they created a small, makeshift firepit. Luke gathered stones and made a circle with them in the clearing.

He then pulled a lighter from his pocket, hesitating a moment before lighting a corner of the letter before tossing it in the homemade firepit. He stood there, watching it burn, and Emma couldn't help but notice tears welling up in his eyes. He blinked them back and cleared his throat. It was the kind of vulnerability she never in a million years expected to see from Luke. Could she blame him, though? After all, his mother had sent him a pretty intense letter after years of silence.

Emma stepped closer to Luke until she was only inches from him. "I'm sorry Luke. I can only imagine what you are going through right now," she said, resting her hand on his shoulder softly for a moment.

He turned toward her, meeting her gaze. "I'm glad you were here for this. I don't think I could have done it alone," Luke said. Emma blinked and tilted her head.

There was one part of the letter she couldn't stop thinking about as they had created the firepit. His mother had told him not to let *anyone* read the letter. Not even his own father. Certainly Emma fell into the category of *anyone*. So why had he let her read it?

"I'm glad you trusted me to read it. But can I ask...why? Your mom seemed pretty adamant about not showing the letter to anyone," Emma whispered.

Luke's gaze intensified, and Emma could feel her heart rate pick up reflexively. "Emma, I do trust you, and that's exactly why you are the only person I knew I could share this with. You are special to me...you know that right?"

Emma was pretty sure her heart was going to jump out of her chest. Luke's words swam around in her head. Special? What did that even mean? She felt her mind drawing conclusions she probably shouldn't. Ones like thinking he thought of her as more than a friend.

Before Emma could think of something to say, she felt Luke's warm hand brushing against hers. His fingertips lightly ran across her palm until his fingers were interlocked with hers. Warmth and electricity shot up her arm in response to his touch. She tried to control her breathing, but that seemed impossible no thanks to her racing heart.

Luke's gaze never broke from hers as they stood there, hand in hand. Emma panicked as she scrambled for something to say to his original question. "Yes," she managed to croak out.

"Good," Luke whispered, his hovering frame so close to her lips that it made her feel dizzy. When did he get so close to her? Emma was almost certain he had never been this close to her before. The feeling of his hand on hers was making reality slip away, and her mind along with it.

"Can I kiss you?" Luke whispered, almost inaudibly.

Her heart hammered wildly at his words. She just stared at him for a moment. Was this real?

"Yes," Emma replied, her voice cracking on the last half of the word.

Luke closed the distance between their lips, brushing them against Emma's. The forest around her faded away and the only thing that was left was Luke's lips lingering softly on hers. His hands cupped her cheeks gently, coaxing her lips to move slowly with his.

Was she doing it right? She had never kissed anyone before, so there was absolutely no way of knowing if she was. But she knew one thing: it *felt* right. One of his hands dropped from her face and wrapped gently around her waist, sending a new shiver up her spine.

They say your first kiss is something you never forget. Emma had never quite understood that. How could something as simple as a boy kissing you for the first time be as life-altering as they say it was? Surely only those boy-crazy girls felt that way, she had thought. Not girls like her. Girls who would rather wake up early and go to a horse show than go to the mall, maybe. But not her.

Not, that is, until she knew what it was like to be kissed by Luke. Luke, who she had sworn only saw her as a friend that he could share his secrets with.

The first time she ever jumped a horse was a memory forever burned in her brain. Nerves, excitement, fear, and the thrill of flying were all mixed up inside her those few seconds between leaving the ground and being airborne. This moment, kissing Luke for the first time, oddly felt *exactly* like that.

Luke continued to kiss her gently, but like he meant it. It made her stomach twist with a pleasure she'd never felt before. Feeling a little braver now, she ran her hand up his arm until it rested on the back of his neck.

In all her sixteen years of life, she had never felt anything like she was feeling in this moment.

Emma wasn't sure how long Luke had been kissing her when he finally pulled slightly away. A small smile tugged at his lips when his gaze met hers, and Emma was sure she was staring at him like a deer in headlights.

As magical as that moment had been, it had been even more unexpected.

"I...I didn't think you thought of me that way," Emma stammered.

"You didn't think I liked you?" Luke replied, seeming surprised.

"I thought you just wanted to be friends," Emma said with a half shrug.

Luke leaned in again, giving her a brief, feather-light kiss. "Think again," he whispered, making the hair raise on her arm.

Emma looked around for the first time in a while, noticing just how dark it was beginning to get in the woods.

"We'd better head back, huh?" Luke said, following her gaze to the darkening sky.

"We probably should," Emma replied reluctantly.

Luke smiled warmly at her and laced his fingers through hers as they began walking down the path towards the barn. Emma found herself smiling the whole way back.

This was definitely not how she expected the evening to go.

However, it was better than she could have ever imagined.

Chapter Ten

Emma felt a little extra bounce in her step as she made her way down the hallway towards her locker. A sappy grin had been plastered semi-permanently on her face since last night, a night that had changed her world forever. At least, that's how she was feeling after her first kiss.

If someone had told her just a few months ago that her first kiss would be with Luke Cromwell, she would have bet everything she had that that would never come true.

But here she was, half-skipping down the hallway like the love-sick teenager she was, after doing exactly that. Emma was starting to understand the way Melissa had acted around Johnny when they first started dating. Melissa had wanted to spend every moment she could with Johnny when she wasn't with her friends. The way she was constantly flirting with him in the halls or gushing about him to her and Kaylin...it had made it that much worse when Johnny dumped Melissa out of the blue.

Emma promised herself not to be like that. Partly because she had other things in her life, like her horse. But in a way, that wasn't really an option. They were still secret friends, after all. Well, friends was a bit of an understatement as of yesterday. Were they secretly dating now? Or had last night's kiss been the biproduct of emotions and proximity?

The sappy grin suddenly fell from Emma's face. Maybe sleeping on it last night had made Luke realize he had made a mistake kissing her. After all, there had been zero talk of being more than friends until last night's unexpected kiss. Sure, he had said something about her being special to him, but friends can be special right? And yes, he had said he liked her, but maybe he had just been wrapped up in moment.

"Good morning," a voice said behind her.

Emma spun around wide-eyed and met Kaylin and Melissa's gazes. She had been so wrapped up in her own thoughts that she hadn't registered the sound of her friends' chatting voices approaching.

"Whoa, you ok? You look...," Melissa began, biting her lip as she trailed off. Between being caught off guard, suddenly realizing the kiss that felt life-altering might have meant nothing to Luke, and the lack of sleep causing dark circles under her eyes...it made sense why Melissa was questioning her frazzled appearance.

I didn't sleep well," Emma replied quickly. That part was true. She had spent hours lying in bed replaying the evening in her mind over and over when she should have been sleeping. But sleep seemed much less relevant than the epic night she had spent with Luke. Besides the fact she had experienced her first kiss, there were also a lot of things about his mother's letter that had her mind spinning with additional questions.

"I'll say. Don't worry, my under eye concealer comes with me every day for emergencies just like this one," Melissa said proudly, pulling the concealer compact from her purse.

"Thanks Mel," Emma replied with a weak smile. How long did she expect to keep all of this from them? Lying to the people she cared about was not something she did, so how on earth had she managed to land herself into such a tangled web of them?

Now, the stakes were even higher. Luke wasn't just her secret friend anymore. He was the boy who had secretly kissed her for the first time. From time to time,

Emma had wondered what that moment would be like. Not that she had dwelled on it too much. She had no real interest in boys, until Luke came along, that is.

Still, the moment had played out in her mind much differently than this. Emma considered blurting it all out right then and there and letting the chips fall where they may. Maybe Melissa and Kaylin would forgive her and understand her motive for the secrecy in the first place. Or maybe she would alienate her only friends, and for what? A kiss that may or may not have been *something?* It may have been her first kiss, but she knew it was far from Luke's first kiss. What it meant to *her* couldn't possibly be the same as what it had meant to *him*.

"Maybe I should wait until I know what this is between us before I tell them," she thought.

It seemed like the best choice at the moment.

Melissa held the mirror portion of her compact up so Emma could see while she dabbed a little of the concealer under her eyes.

"Much better," Melissa said as she scanned Emma's face while she put the compact back in her purse.

Emma smiled warmly at her friends as she fell in step with them walking towards the other side of the school where their class was.

But Emma's mind was already churning over what she needed to do next.

By the end of the school day, Emma felt like she was bursting at the seams. There had not been one good opportunity for her and Luke to exchange notes. Not that she had written one. In fact, she had a pile of crumpled up, half-written notes that would never see the light of day. By the second half of the day, she had come to the conclusion that talking to Luke about the kiss would be something she needed to do in person.

Emma had hoped maybe Luke would have something to say in a note first. At least then she could figure out exactly where his head was. But every time she walked by him in the hall or passed his locker, he had been surrounded by his posse of friends, or worse, Jaclyn and Chad. For fear of having Jaclyn figure out there was something between them, Emma avoided eye contact with Luke altogether, which meant getting an idea of how he felt by his facial expressions wasn't an option.

Now, it was the end of the day, and she was headed to the back student parking lot. Melissa and Kaylin had of course insisted on walking to their cars together, which meant Emma now had a very small window of time between when they drove away and Luke leaving too.

Would he see her and wait for her? Or would he drive off and avoid her because he knew kissing her was a big mistake? Her heart rate picked up its pace as she ran through every possible scenario.

"...and then we should go to dinner before the dance at that cute Italian restaurant down the street from school. What do you think, Emma?" Melissa asked as they walked out of the back doors of the school.

"Yeah, um, that sounds good to me," Emma said, still scanning the parking lot for Luke's truck. Emma's gaze locked onto it at the same time she heard Kaylin start speaking.

"You guys, look! Isn't that Katie, Luke's ex, talking to him? Since when are they an item again?" Kaylin said in a hushed tone.

Emma suddenly felt like she had been punched in the gut. Hard.

Katie lightly flipped a piece of curly blonde hair behind her shoulder as she spoke. Emma was pretty sure she was going to throw up as she watched her lightly swat at Luke's shoulder playfully.

"Ugh, not since that huge blowout break-up in the hallway last year. I'm surprised Katie has the nerve to even talk to him since that day, but hey, it has been a year. Maybe he forgave her?" Melissa replied with a shrug.

"I mean, it doesn't hurt that she's pretty," Kaylin added, shaking her head.

"Like she walked right out of a Neutrogena ad," Melissa said, rolling her eyes too.

Kaylin and Melissa both looked over at Emma as if waiting for her to chime in with her distaste. Before she really knew Luke, she would have had a whole list of commentary for the exchange between the former couple. But now, she was just trying not to throw up in the middle of the parking lot as she watched the two of them talk.

"She is pretty," Emma managed to croak out, her eyes never leaving Luke and Katie as they talked. What was she saying to him? Katie seemed to be giving him an earful. Luke's expression was unreadable from where they were, making her feel more anxious. Was he enjoying the conversation?

"Whatever, those two probably deserve each other anyway. Last time I checked, Luke hasn't dated anyone since her. Maybe he has still been hung up on her all this time," Melissa said with a half shrug.

Emma could feel the blood draining from her face as those words sunk in. She had wondered herself why Luke hadn't dated since Katie. Now, maybe she knew the reason.

"I guess we'll see how *that* drama unfolds. Knowing Katie, there is *sure* to be drama at the dance if she is trying to sink her claws back into Luke," Kaylin said.

Emma purposely turned toward her car a little early so her friends wouldn't see the sickly look on her face.

"See you tomorrow!" Emma said as enthusiastically as she could manage, waving over her shoulder.

"Bye Emma!" Melissa and Kaylin said almost in unison as they walked toward their respective cars.

Emma slid into her car and shut the door, drawing in a slow breath. She reminded herself that Melissa and Kaylin didn't know about Luke kissing her last night, and that maybe they would have a different theory about Luke talking to Katie if that was the case.

Although, the fact that Luke hadn't dated since their break-up still tugged at her mind.

Emma turned on her car and put it into gear as she began to creep forward, her gaze locked on Luke and Katie. She just needed to pull up a little more so she could see Luke's face too as he was talking to her. Maybe then she could see how he felt about...

"Hey! Watch where you're going!" a voice screamed and the rattle of a hand smacking against the hood of her car brought Emma back to reality. She wasn't sure it was possible, but her face became whiter than before.

Jaclyn and Chad were glaring at her through her windshield. It was pretty clear what had happened: she had almost hit them both with her car.

If Emma could list two people who would be the worst to almost run over, it was these two. What's more, she had been staring down Luke and Katie like a stalker when she did. Had Jaclyn seen Emma's panicked expression as she tried to get a better look at Luke?

Emma rolled her window down. "I'm...sorry," Emma spat out. Her sheet white face was now turning beat red.

"Learn how to drive," Jaclyn replied, rolling her eyes as she looped her arm through her boyfriend's and began walking away.

Now Emma was not really sure if she had busted herself. If she had, Jaclyn was surely saving that bomb for later.

Emma shot a quick look over her shoulder at Luke and Katie, who had both turned in her direction now, no doubt interrupted by her screeching tires and Jaclyn's voice echoing across the parking lot. Mortified, Emma looked both ways and pulled out of the parking space as she headed towards the exit.

Emma could not get away fast enough from half the school staring at her, and more importantly, the way Katie was looking at Luke. Fighting the urge be sick yet again, Emma pulled onto the main road and beelined for home.

Emma's stomach was still in knots the next day as she walked into school. She may have been able to run away from her problems yesterday afternoon, but they were right here waiting for her at school today. Snickers and sideways glances from other students told her exactly what she had been dreading: she had caused a scene and everyone was talking about it. Surely Jaclyn had a lot to do with it, if she had to guess.

Couldn't Emma have simply run over someone else? Literally *anyone* else?

Emma knew one thing though, and that was she couldn't mentally survive another day of wondering where she stood with Luke. Anger mixed with fear as she walked purposely down the hallway avoiding the stares and giggles that followed her. Even if the kiss meant nothing to Luke, talking to Katie like that out in the open was downright rude.

All morning as she got ready for school, Emma had formulated a plan in her mind. That plan included the pre-written note that she currently death-gripped in her right hand. She knew that Luke got to school earlier than most of his habitually-late friends, and it might be her only window of opportunity.

Emma slowed her pace as she rounded the corner of the hallway leading to Luke's locker. As predicted, he was swapping his books from his backpack to his locker. Doing a quick scan of the hallway for anyone who might be watching, she made eye contact with Luke before tossing the folded up note in front of him.

Looking over her shoulder briefly, she saw Luke wait until she was a few steps away before picking up. If Emma's emotions hadn't been all over the place, she probably would have smiled to herself at how good they had gotten at discretely exchanging notes. But not today.

Today, she wanted answers, and until she got them, her stomach would continue to be tied in knots.

Emma imagined Luke reading the tiny note as she continued down the hallway. She had written:

L –

Meet me in front of room 106 at 9:30 am.

No thanks to the now heavy suspicion on Jaclyn's part, Emma had recently decided to leave out the *secret friend* part as a precaution. She didn't need any reason for Jaclyn to keep connecting the dots. If Jaclyn saw Luke with a note that was signed by a secret friend, it definitely wouldn't be long before she figured it all out.

Emma figured the best way to be sure no one saw them talking was to have Luke to make up an excuse and ask to leave in the middle of class to meet her. The hallways would be virtually empty, making the odds less likely to be seen by anyone. Waiting until after school would have been torture.

Now, Emma just had to make it through another hour and a half before she got the answers she was so desperate for.

Emma stood in front of room 106, keeping her eyes peeled for hall monitors, teachers, or worse, friends of Luke's.

Checking her watch, she saw Luke was five minutes late. Was he not able to get out of class? Or worse, was he blowing her off completely?

The seconds ticked by slowly as Emma anxiously waited to see if Luke would show up.

Letting out a sigh of relief, she saw Luke round the corner two minutes later.

"Sorry, I had a hard time getting out of class. The teacher made me wait until she had finished covering test material," Luke said in a hushed tone.

"It's ok, follow me," Emma whispered, doing one last scan of the hallway before opening the door behind her.

Luke's eyes went wide as they took in the room. "What is this place?" he asked.

Emma chuckled a little, despite the fact butterflies were doing somersaults in her chest in anticipation of the conversation.

"I said the same thing when Melissa first showed me this room. It's called the green room. Apparently not many students know about it," Emma replied.

Emma sat on the small couch on the other side of the room and Luke followed suit. There was no way she was going to have this conversation standing.

"Luke, I saw you talking to Katie," Emma blurted out. She knew she was stating the obvious. After all, half the school had been talking about it. That, and her almost running Jaclyn over with her car. Although luckily, no one was connecting the two incidents together. Except maybe Jaclyn.

"I figured that might be why you asked me to meet you," Luke replied, his gaze dropping to the ground.

"Do you want to get back together with her?" Emma asked quickly. May as well find that out up front. The rest of the conversation would be pointless of he did.

Luke's eyes widened as he met Emma's. "I kissed *you* two days ago, remember?" Luke replied, a slight smirk forming on his lips.

Of course she remembered. It was all she had thought about since. Luke scooted closer to her on the coach, placing his hand over hers, running her fingertips over the back of her hand.

"So, then, why was Katie...," Emma stammered, biting her lip. His touch was making it hard to think.

Luke let out a breath. "Katie is being Katie. The guy she started dating after we broke up ended things. She was asking if I had a date to the dance this weekend and asked if I wanted to go with her as friends, although I'm sure she has an ulterior motive. She apologized for cheating on me, told me she made a big mistake, and asked for me to forgive her," Luke said.

Emma stopped breathing for a moment. "What did you tell her?" Emma asked breathlessly.

"I told her I forgive her, but that I was going with someone else," Luke replied, still holding her gaze. Emma felt a tightness in her chest. She and Luke couldn't possibly go to a public function like the dance together, so had he asked someone else to go with him instead?

"Who?" Emma asked.

"You," Luke said, his eyes twinkling a little.

"But we can't...," Emma began.

"I figured you would say that. So, I have a plan," Luke said, his face was lit up now.

"What is it?" Emma asked, leaning in closer reflexively.

"It's a surprise," Luke replied.

Emma tilted her head curiously as she studied his expression. The look on his face told her she wasn't getting any more answers about that today. Still, she felt a warmth spreading through her at the thought of whatever plan Luke was cooking up.

Emma's gaze dropped to the ground as she thought about the other question she hadn't asked. "I thought maybe you wanted to get back together with Katie since you haven't dated anyone else since the two of you broke up. I guess I'm just wondering...why?"

Luke had said in so many words he didn't want to get back together with Katie, but still, the fact that he hadn't dated since tugged at Emma's mind. She dared to look at Luke again, whose face had scrunched up a bit.

"Katie really did a number on me. I guess after that, I was a little hesitant to date anyone else. No one I've talked to since has pushed me to want to open up to anyone else again," Luke said, pausing.

Emma felt Luke's gaze intensify as he looked at her.

"That is, until I started becoming friends with you," Luke added.

Emma thought her heart might beat right out of her chest. Was Luke really admitting he liked her the way she liked him? She felt her jaw begin to drop but slammed it shut. A thousand things she could say back swirled around her mind, but none of them felt right. There was really only one thing that felt right, actually.

Emma leaned in further, closing the gap between them. Letting her instincts take the lead, she softly brushed her lips against Luke's the way she remembered him doing. Her hand slowly wound around his neck, her fingertips lightly ran across his soft skin. His lips were moving slowly with hers now, sending the butterflies in her chest into overdrive.

His arm wound around her back, pulling her a little closer. She wasn't sure how long they had been lost in that kiss, but a student walking past the doorway in the hall talking to someone else pulled her back to reality.

They both pulled away reluctantly at the sound.

"We'd better get back to class before someone misses us," Emma said in a hushed tone.

"We probably should," Luke agreed, standing up now and offering his hand to Emma to help her up. Emma was pulled to her feet and found herself standing close to Luke when she did.

"See you later," Luke murmured, lightly kissing her on the cheek before he turned towards the door.

"See you," Emma mumbled.

She waited an extra thirty seconds after Luke left before leaving the room and heading back to class herself.

A sappy grin tugged at her lips as she walked down the hall replaying the last few minutes in her mind.

***

Emma held her black and white ballgown-style prom dress in one hand as she climbed awkwardly out of Melissa's car.

"You guys, I can't believe we are finally at the spring dance!" Melissa exclaimed, clasping her hands together.

"Me either!" Kaylin chimed in, beaming.

Emma watched as other students made their way to the front door of the school in formal wear. She wondered if Luke was already here, and what exactly the surprise was that he had planned. He hadn't given up any hints the rest of the week despite her prying. All he kept saying was to go to the punch bowl and wait for him to slip her a note.

They walked through the decorated entryway and paused to smile for a group picture in front of the backdrop.

"I wonder if Johnny is here," Melissa said, a slight frown crossing her face. Emma rested her hand on her friend's shoulder. "Don't think about him tonight, ok? I'm sure he will see how stunning you look in this dress and remember what an idiot he was."

"You deserve better than what he did to you," Kaylin added.

"Thanks guys," Melissa said with a sad smile.

The thought had crossed Emma's mind while they were at dinner to just come right out and tell her friends about Luke. After all, she now knew he had feelings for her. But after Melissa spent half of dinner reminiscing on how she and Johnny had talked about going to the dance together before they broke up, or how heartbroken she would be if she saw him dancing with another girl, Emma decided it wasn't the best time. Melissa was already in a fragile state tonight as it was. No use rubbing her newfound happiness with Luke in her friend's face.

"Come on, let's dance!" Kaylin said, grabbing Emma and Melissa's hands as she drug them onto the dance floor. Emma eyed the table with the punch bowl. No Luke yet. Unless he was somewhere here already, hidden in the crowd waiting for her to go up there. He hadn't exactly said how early or late in the evening to go to the punch table. Was she supposed to go up there when she first arrived?

Well, there was no way she was getting out of dancing with Melissa and Kaylin anytime soon. Plus, Melissa was already looking happier as she twirled around the dance floor with her friends at her side. Melissa needed her right now, so Luke would simply have to wait.

Emma wasn't sure how long the three of them had been on the dance floor, but she did know she found herself lost in singing the words to every song as she danced with her friends, losing all track of time.

"I'm going to grab some punch. I'll be right back," Emma said.

"Ok!" Melissa said, laughing as she and Kaylin began dancing to the next song.

By now, Luke was probably starting to wonder where she was. She and her friends had found themselves deep in the crowd, surrounded by other students on the dance floor, and Emma hadn't seen Luke or his friends once.

Emma moved through the crowd as she made her way to the punch table. She slowly poured some of the punch into a paper cup as she did a quick glance around the room for Luke.

She stood there, taking long drinks and hoping Luke had a chance to spot her. Right around the time she thought about heading back to the dance floor, she saw Luke emerge from the other side of the dance floor.

Emma dropped her gaze and tried to hide the smile forming on her lips. Luke casually walked up beside her and set a small folded up note on the table before filling his cup with punch and walking away.

Grabbing the note, Emma slipped away and headed to the back of the room so she could read it.

E –

Meet me at my locker in five minutes.

Emma felt her heart beat faster in her chest.

Five minutes? There was no way she was going to be able to find her friends on the dance floor and make it to Luke's locker across the building in five minutes. Well, whatever he had planned couldn't possibly take that long. She would just tell her friends she had to use the restroom or something when she made it back to them.

Walking down the halls, Emma passed several couples who had decided to use the empty hallways as a place to talk privately. Some were so lost in a kiss they didn't even know she had passed them.

Excitement flooded her as she walked down the hallway that led to the one where Luke's locker was located. She still hadn't been able to figure out exactly what he could have planned, especially now that she knew it was at his locker, since there weren't a lot of options there.

But as Emma rounded the corner and got her first glance at Luke's set-up, she felt herself suck in a breath of surprise.

Luke stood in his black suit and tie next to a small speaker playing a slow George Strait song. Two lit candles were on either side of it. He was grinning from ear to ear when he saw her.

"Emma Walker, may I have this dance?" Luke asked. He had one hand behind his back and the other outstretched toward her.

"Luke...this is incredible!" Emma stammered. She took his hand and Luke immediately spun her around in a circle before pulling her in, making Emma laugh.

Luke's arms twisted around her back and she rested both hands on his chest. They moved slowly in circles as they danced to "Carrying Your Love With Me."

Luke gently pushed her back, spinning her around twice before dipping her, his arms catching her as she neared the ground. "Luke Cromwell, you did not tell me you knew how to dance," Emma said with wide eyes, smiling.

His lips twitched into a sad smile. "Mom taught me. This was one of her favorite songs, actually. She used to make my dad dance with her in the kitchen every time it came on the radio," Luke replied.

Luke planted her back on her feet, pulling her close again. Emma rested her chin on Luke's shoulder as they continued to dance slowly.

"Well now, isn't this interesting. I thought I heard your voice, Luke, but this is the *last* person I expected you to be with."

Emma felt her heart sinking the moment she recognized the voice. For a moment, she considered not turning around and instead running the other way. Not that it would do her any good. They had been spotted dancing, and there was nothing running away could do to cover that up.

Emma felt Luke's hands fall from her waist to his sides and she slowly turned around.

There Jaclyn Alcott stood, her arms crossed over her chest, wearing a fitted, mermaid-style, red sequin dress. She looked stunning in it despite the venomous look on her face. The moment Emma had dreaded might happen since she and Luke became secret friends was glaring her right in the face.

"I've got to say, Emma, I didn't expect *this* to be your secret boyfriend," Jaclyn said with one eyebrow raised. A smirk was tugging at her lips. She had interrupted them in the middle of a moment that was impossible for Emma to talk her way out of, and she knew it.

"Luke isn't my... I mean we weren't...," Emma stammered, biting her lip. Well, she wasn't exactly sure what they were, but there was no good way to dig herself out of this.

"Jaclyn, there you...," Chad stopped talking when he rounded the corner, a surprised look on his face when he took in a wide-eyed Emma and Luke standing side by side next to an obviously romantic setup.

"Whoa, Luke, I didn't know you and Emma were...," Chad paused again, seeming unsure of what to say next.

An awkward, heavy silence fell between them for what felt like forever, but Emma knew it had probably only been a few seconds. She was still scrambling to think of something to say, but really, what could possibly be said that would reverse this kind of damage? Nothing.

"Jaclyn, don't make a big deal out of this," Luke snapped back, slipping his fingers through Emma's.

Emma felt heat in her cheeks as she watched the smirk on Jaclyn's face grow wider. Of course, she assumed Luke's public display of affection was the reason.

"Emma?"

Cringing, Emma turned around to another familiar voice. Melissa and Kaylin were standing there, and the look on their faces felt like a knife to the heart.

Kaylin looked from Emma and Luke to Jaclyn and Chad. "We got worried when you didn't come back from getting punch, so we came looking for you. We heard you talking to Jaclyn and thought...," Kaylin trailed off, her gaze darting back to Emma and Luke again.

"What's going on Emma?" Melissa asked, her eyes narrowing as she stared at Luke's fingers intertwined with Emma's. Emma felt like her face was on fire now and dropped her hand from Luke's.

"Melissa, I can explain...," Emma pleaded.

"Explain what, Em? How you and Luke had a moment after he shared his family secrets with you, blew you off, and then suddenly you became...this!" Melissa motioned to Emma and Luke. "Then, you think it's ok to lie to us about it for who knows how long? Clearly *Jaclyn* of all people knew before we did! Friends don't lie to each other about something like this, Emma!"

Emma felt tears welling in her eyes. She could practically feel Jaclyn's gaze boring holes into her, but she didn't dare turn around. Everything Jaclyn had predicted about how her friends would react was coming true right in front of her.

Luke turned to Emma with hurt in his eyes. "You told them about my family? You promised you wouldn't," Luke said under his breath.

A tear spilled over onto her cheek. "Not everything, I just...," her voice broke, and she swallowed hard against the tightness in her throat.

Everyone was staring at her, looks ranging from anger and confusion on her friends' and Luke's faces, to the "I told you so" look on Jaclyn's.

"Come on Luke, let's get out of here," Jaclyn said, taking Chad's hand as they headed down the hallway back towards the dance. Luke held Emma's gaze for another few moments, the betrayal there was unmistakable. Then, he turned around and followed Chad and Jaclyn.

Emma turned back toward her friends. "I know I should have told you...," Emma began.

"Emma, I don't want to talk about this tonight. Find your own ride home, ok?" Melissa said as she turned on her heels. Kaylin shot Emma a sad look before following behind Melissa.

Emma stood there alone in the hallway, tears streaming down her face. She knew this could happen. She knew it from the moment she and Luke made the secret friendship pact in the first place.

But Emma hadn't expected a fallout quite like this.

Chapter Eleven

The fallout of the spring dance haunted Emma for the rest of what was left of the weekend. She wasn't exactly sure what to expect when she arrived at school that morning, but she found she was *completely* shut out by the people she cared about most.

Melissa and Kaylin had simply given her a sideways look and walked past her locker. Emma would have taken a knockdown, drag out fight over the cold shoulder they were giving her. At least that meant they were talking to her.

Luke had avoided eye contact the one time she passed him in the hall, confirming her suspicions that things might just go back to the way they were when Luke pretended she didn't exist.

The moment school was over for the day, Emma ran to the one thing that always made things a little better: her horse.

Emma pressed her forehead against Lexington's soft forelock and felt tears stinging in her eyes for what felt like the hundredth time since the dance.

How could she have been so stupid? She knew lying to her friends would have consequences, and now she was paying for it.

And then there was Luke. This was the exact reason she had stayed far away from boys before. Emma wasn't sure if the pain of losing Luke was worth everything she had felt when they were together. At least, not in this moment.

Emma tugged gently at the lead rope as she walked her horse out of the barn towards one of the open pastures. She was sure that if she had tried riding today, it would have just gone poorly. Horses pick up on their riders' emotions easily, and her emotions were out of control.

Instead, she opted for letting her horse hand graze while she pondered a way to put her life back together. That is, if her friends ever forgave her.

It had been a long, lonely week at school.

Her friends had continued to give her the cold shoulder, and Luke... well, Luke seemed to be avoiding her.

Now, it was Friday, and she was in her last class of the day. Emma couldn't remember a time she wanted to leave school for the weekend more than today. Still, this should have been the kind weekend she was excited about. After all, you only turn seventeen once.

The bell rang, signaling her longest week of school ever was finally over. Emma walked quickly toward her locker, ready to put it behind her.

But Emma was surprised to see Melissa and Kaylin leaning against her locker, waiting for her.

"Um, hey guys," Emma stammered. After a week of radio silence, what finally made them approach her? Was this the part where they ripped into her again?

"Hey Emma," Melissa said quietly.

Emma's gaze darted from Melissa to Kaylin as she desperately tried to read their expressions.

"Listen, what you did was a pretty crappy friend move, but we still know what tomorrow is," Kaylin said.

"Don't think this means you're off the hook for what you did, but we have all been friends too long to let it end like this," Melissa chimed in.

Emma raised an eyebrow. What exactly were they saying?

"I wish I could go back and do everything differently, you know," Emma replied, her gaze dropping to the floor.

"We figured you might say that," Melissa said, a smile tugging at her lips.

"So, does this mean you guys don't hate me anymore?" Emma asked.

"Em, we never hated you; we were just hurt that you lied to us," Kaylin said.

"Trust me, I see the logic of why you did it. I mean, dating Luke Cromwell in secret?" Melissa shook her head, chuckling a little.

"You're definitely going to have to fill us in on everything you have been keeping a secret," Kaylin said, smiling now too.

"Well, there isn't much to tell now. Luke hasn't even looked my way since the dance. I broke a promise to him too, and it looks like he hasn't forgiven me quite so easily," Emma said.

"That's probably our fault," Melissa said, shooting a look at Kaylin.

"I don't blame either of you. I made a mess of the whole situation," Emma said, feeling the tightness in her throat coming back.

Melissa looped her arm through Emma's. "Well, we will be sure you have the best seventeenth birthday ever anyway. So good, you won't even *think* about Luke Cromwell."

"Thanks Mel," Emma said with a weak smile.

The three of them walked down the hallway towards the school exit.

Luke may be out of her life for good now, but at least she could face it with her best friends at her side again.

Melissa had been right; Emma was having so much fun that she had moments where she forgot all about Luke. The weather had even decided to cooperate, making for a perfect almost summer-like seventy-four degree, clear sky after-noon.

Melissa squealed as she ran through where the underground pop-up fountains launched water up sporadically, knowing she could be blasted with one at any moment. Although, that was half the fun of this game.

Emma was already soaking wet and laughing until she couldn't breathe as she stood alongside Kaylin and watched Melissa get pelted in the arm with a blast of water that came up on her right side.

"Ok, playing Russian roulette in the fountains *was* a good idea," Emma said breathlessly. She hadn't laughed this hard since things went south with Luke.

"I know, I was skeptical when Melissa suggested it, but this has been a blast," Kaylin replied.

After lunch at Emma's favorite restaurant, the group had headed to this outdoor mall to shop, and apparently, to run through the pop-up fountains.

Melissa sat on the bench beside Emma and Kaylin as she caught her breath. "I got blasted in the back too right before I made it out," Melissa said, smiling. The warm breeze blew through their clothes, slowly drying them out.

Emma suddenly caught her breath, her eyes narrowing. "What is *she* doing here?" Emma said.

Jaclyn Alcott was walking across the street directly toward where they were sitting. Was it not enough Jaclyn had ruined her relationship with Luke? Did she really need to ruin her birthday too?

"Emma, I know this is going to sound crazy, but I think you need to hear her out," Melissa said.

Emma's eyes widened as she shot Melissa a look of surprise. "I'm sorry, did you just say I should *hear Jaclyn out*?" Emma said, her jaw dropping.

"I told you it was going to sound crazy. Listen, I don't typically trust Jaclyn as far as I can throw her, but this time, I think you'll want to hear what she has to say," Melissa replied.

Emma just stared at Melissa, processing. "Are you telling me you *invited* her here?"

"Yes," was all Melissa had time to say before Jaclyn was standing in front of them.

Jaclyn chuckled a little. "You guys look like wet cats," she said, smiling.

Emma wasn't sure if she meant it as an insult or not, but since it was Jaclyn, she was going to assume the former.

Jaclyn's gaze shifted to Emma. "Can I talk to you privately, Emma?"

Emma tossed one last confused look at Melissa before standing up. She was too curious to not see what Jaclyn had to say. Whatever it was, it was clearly important enough to have Melissa's blessing. Unless she had fooled Melissa too, which wouldn't surprise her.

Jaclyn sat on a bench across the way from where Melissa and Kaylin were. She blew out a breath before turning toward Emma. "Look, I'm sure I'm the last person you expected to talk to today. Happy birthday, by the way," Jaclyn said.

"Thanks," Emma murmured.

"I know it's been awhile since we were friends, and I know that's my fault. Getting wrapped up in the world of popularity is easy. When I started dating Chad, I felt like I had to be *one of them*, you know? So I shut you, Melissa, and Kaylin out. I thought being friends with you all still would somehow make Chad and the rest of his friends like me less. Then, as time went on, I didn't even recognize myself anymore. But it was too late, you know? It was like it was my new identity. I'm telling you all this because I've been thinking the last few days that maybe that's exactly what was happening to you. You got tangled in all those secrets and lies and then suddenly, you didn't know how you got to where you are now."

Emma hated to admit it, but Jaclyn was right.

"That's pretty much how it happened," Emma replied.

"Yeah, I thought so. There's something else you should know. The reason I've been such a witch to you is because, honestly Emma, I've been jealous of you for a long time."

Emma's eyes widened. "I'm sorry...did you just say you've been jealous of *me*?" How on earth was that possible?

"Oh please Emma, you have to know how naturally pretty you are. You have way more going for you than you give yourself credit for. Almost every time you walk past us in the hallway, the guys in our group make some sort of comment. Even Chad has before," Jaclyn said, her eyes dropping to the ground. Emma saw a pained look in them before she did.

"Anyway, I thought you should know all that. There's one other thing, too. Luke is miserable. I mean, he hasn't come right out and said anything to us, but it's *so* obvious. Emma, he's crazy about you. Honestly, I think he's liked you for a while now."

Emma tilted her head. "Why do you say that?"

"Oh please, the way he's looked at you for like, the last year, it doesn't take a rocket scientist to see that," Jaclyn said, rolling her eyes but smiling a little.

Emma shook her head in disbelief. "You know Jac, maybe Chad isn't the best guy for you if he's blatantly making comments about other girls right in front of you. I mean, I can't imagine it's just me, right?"

"No, it isn't. But if I dump him...," Jaclyn trailed off, not looking up.

"You think that's it for being popular and being friends with all of them, don't you?" Emma guessed.

"Pretty much," Jaclyn replied.

Emma wrapped an arm around Jaclyn's shoulder. "If you do decide to leave him, I'll be here for you," Emma replied, smiling warmly.

"Thanks, Emma. He's not so bad, really, but if the day ever comes, you'll be the first to know" Jaclyn said, returning her smile. "You should really talk to Luke, though."

Emma scrunched up her nose. "I doubt he wants to talk to me. He has been avoiding me all week. Honestly, I think I just need to face facts. I screwed things up big time, and Luke is never going to forgive me for it."

"I wouldn't be so sure about that," Jaclyn said, a mischievous smile crossed her face and she looked over her shoulder at an area across the street near some shops. Emma followed Jaclyn's gaze, turning around on the bench until she was sure her eyes weren't playing tricks on her.

There, standing with his hands in his pockets was Luke, looking right at her. Emma spun back around to look at Jaclyn again. "Did you do this?"

"I talked to Luke and made him see he was being childish. I know how much he likes you, and I reminded him of exactly that. It didn't take too much convincing," Jaclyn said half struggling, but the smile on her face gave away she was proud of her meddling.

Emma was just glad that this time her meddling was actually to her benefit. It was almost hard to believe, but Jaclyn was acting like, dare she even think it, a friend again?

"Jac, can I ask...why the change of heart? No offense, but this is the *last* thing I expected from *you*," Emma asked.

"I saw the way you moped around the halls of school all alone this week. It was hard to miss," Jaclyn said with a smirk. "I guess for some reason, it made me think about when we were friends once. I figured I tortured you enough for one year. May as well make it up to you a little," Jaclyn said, shrugging, trying to sound nonchalant.

"Thank you," Emma replied with a weak smile.

Jaclyn stood up and put her hands on her hips. "Well, what are you waiting for? I didn't drag him all the way out here for nothing! Go

Emma tossed a quick, appreciative smile to Jaclyn before turning to walk across the street towards Luke. She was suddenly aware again of her damp hair and wet shirt that still clung to her figure. *Of course* this is what she would look like by the time Luke and Jaclyn arrived.

He met her gaze with a shy smile.

"Hey Emma," he whispered when she approached.

"Hey Luke," she replied.

"Want to take a walk?" he offered.

"I'd like that."

Luke led the way around the corner of the outdoor mall until they reached a quiet area with some benches and trees.

"Sorry, we were running through the pop-up fountains," Emma said, squeezing a little water from her damp locks.

"It looks like you had fun," Luke said with a smile, tucking a piece of hair behind her ear. Emma felt her cheeks flush in response to his fingers on her skin. It seemed strange to think it had been a week since she had last felt his touch. Oddly, it felt like no time had passed at all.

"We did," she replied quietly.

Luke cleared his throat, dropping his gaze. "Emma I've been a real jerk this week. I was hurt, and I was angry, but I still should have had a conversation with you about it. But instead I took the easy way out by ignoring you. I know it's going to sound like a cop-out, but I think I may still have some trust issues from Katie that I took out on you, which wasn't fair."

"Luke, I was the one who was wrong. I made you a promise and I broke it. It was at a point when I thought maybe our friendship was over, so I told Melissa and Kaylin about your dad and the way he reacted to you the day he caught you riding. I'm so sorry."

"So, you didn't tell them about my mother? Or the letter? Not that I blame you after the way I acted this week," Luke asked, his gaze dropping to the ground.

"Of course not. I know how important that is to you. I made you a promise, and this time, I kept it a secret. I won't make that mistake again," Emma said, her gaze meeting his again.

Luke laced his fingers through Emma's, making her heart rate pick up. "Forgive me?"

"Only if you forgive me too," Emma replied.

Luke leaned in, answering her question by pressing his lips lightly against hers. "I missed you, Em," he murmured, his lips still on hers.

"I missed you too, Luke," she replied. A shiver ran up her spine as his lips gently covered hers again. Emma found herself getting lost in the kiss that took her breath away.

Despite how grim things looked yesterday, it had turned out to be the best seventeenth birthday imaginable.

Chapter Twelve

Emma saw Luke leaning against his truck in the parking lot when she pulled in. Her heart fluttered in response to seeing him waiting for her. It felt odd after all this time of hiding their friendship. But the secret was out now, and with a reconciliation between her friends under her belt, Emma realized there was simply no reason for Luke not to wait for her in the school parking lot.

After all, that's what boyfriends do. Still, Emma could hardly control the grin that stretched across her face as she walked across the parking lot towards Luke.

"Good morning," he said, kissing her on the cheek.

"Good morning," Emma replied.

Luke covered her hand in his, giving it a squeeze. "Ready?" he asked, turning towards the back door of the school.

"Ready," Emma replied, a sappy smile still plastered on her face.

They walked hand in hand up the stairs and Luke opened the door for her, taking her hand again when he had walked through as well.

Emma felt like every eye was on them as they walked down the hallway, clearly showing off their couple status. She had seen countless couples walk through school with their fingers laced through each other's, sharing a kiss now and then. It always had her rolling her eyes and avoiding them any chance she got.

But here she was, *one of them.* Oddly, it felt much different than it had appeared from the outside looking in. But Emma figured that had to do with the person whose hand was wrapped in hers.

"Hey Luke, Emma," Jaclyn said as she passed them, her arm looped through Chad's. Chad high-fived Luke as they passed by. Emma still wasn't sure if she could ever regain the same friendship with Jaclyn after all the bad blood between them, and she still didn't trust her as far as she could throw her, but at least now they weren't sworn enemies anymore.

Luke walked Emma to her locker where Melissa and Kaylin were already waiting for her. "Next time, have our girl dropped off five minutes earlier, ok?" Melissa said, winking at Luke.

"Yes ma'am," Luke responded playfully. He gave Emma a quick kiss on the cheek before heading in the direction of his own locker.

"See you at lunch," he called over his shoulder.

"See you," Emma said back, watching him walk away.

Melissa made a snort-laugh sound. "Oh, I know that look. Emma Walker, you got it *bad* for Luke!"

"Hmm? What? Got what?" Emma replied, only half-listening.

"Exactly," Melissa teased.

Emma exchanged her books at her locker, and then Melissa and Kaylin walked with her towards their first classes of the day.

"I'm glad you're happy Emma," Kaylin said.

"Thanks Kaylin. I am. Luke is the best," Emma replied.

"I guess since all the drama is over, I may as well tell you guys Johnny and I got back together," Melissa said, looking over at Emma, then Kaylin.

Kaylin's eyes widened. "You *what?*"

"I know, it's a bit of a surprise...," Melissa trailed off, biting her lip. Emma remembered the way Melissa and Johnny used to look at each other. It was the same way she looked at Luke. She and Luke had their fair share of bumps in the road to get to this point. Could she blame Melissa for giving Johnny another chance?

"I'm happy for you, Mel. But how did it happen?" Emma asked.

"Actually, it happened at the dance. I ran into him after everything happened with you and Luke in the hallway, and we got to talking. We ended up talking every day this week, and he apologized for running when things got serious. He said he'd never felt that way for anyone and it scared him. So, as of last night when we hung out, he asked me if I wanted to get back together with him. And I said yes," Melissa replied. She still seemed to be scanning her friends' expressions for approval.

"Well Melissa, I'm glad something good came out of that night," Emma said. It felt good to know that night had at least ended up bringing two people back together.

"Thanks Em. I guess I have you to thank because Johnny thought I hated him for ending things, and I doubt he would have said anything to me if it weren't for how upset I looked and what happened that night."

Emma reached out and wrapped an arm around her friend's shoulder. "It sounds like everything turned out the way it was supposed to for both of us."

Emma scanned the cafeteria for Luke, but still didn't see him.

"You guys haven't seen Luke, have you?" Emma asked Kaylin and Melissa.

"Not since this morning. There's no way he's still in class at this point, so he has to be here somewhere around here," Melissa said, setting her tray down on the table.

"I'll be right back," Emma said, setting her tray down before heading across the cafeteria. Maybe he was still in line for food. Pushing open the door to the hallway, Emma scanned the remaining line of people waiting to get food. Still no Luke.

Emma headed out of the cafeteria and down the hallway. If she didn't see him by his locker, she would have to assume he went home for some reason. But why? If he was sick, wouldn't he have said something?

On her way to Luke's locker, Emma passed her own. She stopped, doubling back. What was that sticking out of her locker? Getting closer, she noticed a small piece of paper shoved almost all the way into the slit of her locker door.

Pulling it out, she quickly opened it and read the wrinkled page.

E –

Something is wrong. I'm sorry I had to leave without telling you in person, but you were at lunch already by the time I looked for you. I didn't want anyone else asking questions, so I decided to leave you a note instead.

I know you typically don't skip school, but can you meet me at the Beulah Park racetrack? Don't tell anywhere where you're going.

I'll wait for you at the front gate until 1:00 pm.

- L

Emma reread the words one more time. A chill ran up her spine as she considered his words. Luke wouldn't just leave in the middle of the day like this if it wasn't serious. But why the racetrack? What could be so urgent there?

A million questions raced through her mind as she turned the lock until her locker popped open. Pulling a notebook from the shelf, she ripped a sheet of paper and began scribbling words on it.

M & K –

I had to leave school. I'm fine, and I'll explain later.

- E

Emma shoved the note into the slot in Melissa's locker since it was closest to hers. She checked her watch, realizing she needed to leave now if she had any chance of making it to the track before 1:00 pm.

Picking her backpack off the floor, Emma sprinted down the hallway towards the back door of the school.

Luke needed her, and she would just have to deal with the consequences of leaving school later.

Emma shut the door to her car and briskly walked across the large racetrack parking lot. The clock on her car's dashboard read 12:59 pm when she pulled in.

It still didn't seem to make sense why Luke was here, of all places. This track wasn't completely unfamiliar to Emma. She had not only watched some of the horse races here with Maggie and other riders from her barn, but Maggie had purchased retired racehorses directly from this track as well.

Was there a horse in trouble here? It had been a scenario she circled back to once or twice on her drive over. Sure, Luke still had a soft spot for horses, but would he need to leave school midday to get one? She supposed he would if it was some sort of emergency.

The front gate was in sight now but still no Luke. Emma checked her watch which read 1:01 pm. Swearing under her breath, she was running now. If Luke had just gone in thinking she wasn't coming, maybe she could still find him.

Jogging through the front gate, her eyes scanned the open area for Luke. A blonde-haired male figure rounding the corner caught her eye.

"Luke!" she called out, running breathlessly in the figure's direction. As she rounded the corner, she almost smacked directly into him.

"Emma?" Luke's startled voice said, steadying her by placing both hands on either side of her shoulders.

Emma threw her arms around his neck, breathing out a sigh of relief. "I didn't think I was going to make it! I got your note, but I knew it was going to be close."

"I'm glad you're here," Luke replied. Something about his voice was off though, and it suddenly made her feel unsettled.

Emma pulled away, her hands still wrapped around the back of his neck as she looked him in the eye. "Luke, *what* is going on? Why are we here?" she asked, looking around nervously now.

Luke's eyes reflected the same unsettled look she was feeling.

"Let's find somewhere private," Luke said, taking her hand. He led the way until they found a spot away from the main entrance.

"I got another letter from my mom," Luke said. He pulled out the envelope and handed it to her, but this time, Emma noticed it didn't have any postage on it.

Emma looked up at Luke. "No postage?"

"It was delivered to me at school, and it gets weirder," he said, pointing to the letter

Emma opened the envelope and pulled the piece of paper from it.

Dear Luke,

I need to see you. I can't stand being away from you anymore.

Meet me in the area behind the furthest back barns.

Mom

Emma looked up after reading the letter with a quizzical expression. "Your mom is *here*?"

"See, that's the problem. I don't think she is."

Emma tilted her head. "Why not?"

"Some things aren't adding up. For starters, why would my mom send me a letter not so long ago telling me how she had to leave to keep me safe and had to stay hidden and then all of a sudden show up to see me?"

"Maybe it's safe now?" Emma suggested.

Luke shook his head. "The timing is just too strange. Plus, this isn't exactly like my mom's handwriting. I almost didn't catch it, but it's just a little off. That, and the way it's worded just doesn't sound like mom either. I think it's a fake."

"But why would someone do something like this? And who? Your dad?"

"I doubt it's dad. We have our issues, but he would never do something like this. Plus, I didn't tell him about the original letter. But whoever it is, I think they know my mom."

"So then, who *could* it be?" Emma asked.

"I have no idea," Luke said, the space between his eyes scrunching up.

"Well, there is only one way to find out, right?" Emma said.

"Right," Luke agreed, shoving the letter into his back pocket. They started walking towards the back side of the barns.

"Luke, why do you think the letter had you come here, of all places?"

"Mom used to come here a lot. Actually, it's where my dad and mom met back in the day. Mom was here at least once a month buying Thoroughbreds that she would retrain and then resell once they were ready. Dad used to be an assistant trainer here before they got married and started the farm we have now."

"So this place had meaning for both your parents. This *is* getting weird."

"I know. I can't wrap my head around why, though. I'm glad you're here, Emma. I don't think I could do this alone."

Emma squeezed Luke's hand. "I left school the minute I knew you needed me."

Luke smiled warmly at Emma before turning his attention back on the barns ahead of them. They kept to the far outside of the barns, trying not to draw attention to themselves.

Finally, they reached the barn furthest back on the property where the letter stated his mother would be. Emma and Luke turned to one another, exchanging a worried look.

"Luke, let me look first. Whoever it is will be expecting you, not me, right?"

Luke didn't look convinced. "I don't know Em, it could be dangerous...,"

Emma kissed Luke on the cheek and then walked as quickly as she could away from him and towards the backside of the barn. He may be afraid to put her in danger, but Luke clearly forgot she was a horse girl. And horse girls are not so easily scared off. Had he not ever ridden a chestnut mare? Surely whatever was around that corner couldn't be as scary as riding a fire-breathing dragon.

Emma felt her jaw begin to drop but she shut it quickly as she took in the sight in front of her as she emerged from the side of the barn.

"Play it cool!" she reminded herself.

"Oh, I'm sorry, I must be lost," she said to the lean, blonde-haired man hunched against the barn's siding. Something about him made her stomach turn.

"What are you doing back here?" he asked, his eyes running over her. His words and the way he said them had her mind screaming one thing: run.

"I'm just, um...," she began, backing up, but he was on his feet already, closing the gap between them. Before she had time to turn on her heels, his hand was firmly wrapped around her wrist.

"Who are you!" he demanded.

"He knows!" her mind screamed. Clearly she wasn't as good of a liar as she thought. At least, not when it came to this guy.

"Let go of her!" Luke's voice said behind her.

The man's face went from surprise to a satisfied grin when he saw Luke. "You must be Luke. I take it you sent your little girlfriend here to spy on me first? Clever."

Luke clenched his hands into fist. "I'm not saying anything else until you let go of her."

The man still had a venomous look on his face as he held his hands in the air, releasing Emma. She stumbled back, all but falling into Luke's arms. Luke grabbed Emma's hand, steading her. He began turning around the second she was safely at his side again. It was clear he was ready to get out of there.

"Not so fast, Luke. Don't you want to know where your mother is?"

Luke paused, like he wasn't sure what to do. He turned around slowly, meeting the man's gaze. "How do you know my mother?" Luke demanded.

"That's not important right now. What is important is that your mother is back in town, and if you ever want to see her again, then I wouldn't walk away if I were you."

Luke's face turned white as a ghost. His gaze was intently fixated on the man, an array of emotions crossing his face. Emma squeezed Luke's hand, and he seemed to come back to reality.

"I'm listening," Luke said.

"Good. Now, before you go running off and talking to every cop or security guard on the grounds, just know if you do, mommy is definitely never coming home. Got it?"

Emma watched as Luke swallowed hard, then nodded.

"I'm glad we have an understanding. My, you do look like her, don't you?" the man said.

"What do you want?" Luke asked, his face was starting to turn red now.

"I want a lot of things. But for starters, I want to know how old you are."

Luke looked over at Emma, who had the same confused expression on her face.

"You want to know my age?" Luke paused, still seeming confused. "Why do you want to know...,"

"Do you want to know where your mother is or not?" the man said, cutting Luke off.

"I'm seventeen."

The man's face lit up, like this information somehow excited him.

"What kind of sick and twisted person is this?" Emma thought.

"That is interesting. So many secrets your mother has kept from you," the man said, almost like he was talking to himself.

"Tell me where my mother is," Luke demanded.

The man's face fell into a frown. "Did you really think answering one question would be enough for me to tell you where she is?"

Luke didn't respond; he only grimaced in the man's direction.

"You know, your mother caused me a lot of pain. Don't you think someone needs to pay for that?"

"My mother wouldn't hurt *anyone*!" Luke said, taking two steps back.

Emma suddenly felt Luke tugging on her hand in the opposite direction.

"Run, Emma!" Luke yelled, pulling her along as he sprinted off.

Emma felt a jolt of adrenaline rush through her as she sprinted behind Luke towards the front gate of the track. At one point, she tried to look over her shoulder, hoping the man wasn't following them. She didn't think he was chasing them, but she wasn't planning to pause long enough to get a good look.

They didn't stop running until they reached Luke's truck, panting heavily. Emma scanned the parking lot for the man but didn't see him. Luke was also running his eyes over the lot.

"I don't see him," Emma said.

"I think we lost him," Luke agreed.

His arm wrapped around her waist and he pulled her in. "I shouldn't have asked to come. You shouldn't have been wrapped up in all of this...,"

Emma put one finger on his lips, removing it only to kiss him sweetly. "We're in this together now, and I'm fine, ok? We will figure this out." She smiled as reassuringly as she could despite the fact she was still rattled inside.

"Let's get out of here. I'll follow you home, ok?"

"Ok," Emma agreed.

Sliding into her car, Emma felt the adrenaline begin to wear off as she processed what had just happened.

Who was this man, and what did he want from Luke? And more importantly, was Luke's mother really in danger?

Emma watched as Luke walked around school in a daze since the day they met that man at the racetrack. It had been two days since, and it was like he was waiting for the other shoe to drop. And in a way, that's exactly what was happening.

"Did I make the right choice running away? Should I have stood my ground to see if the man would lead me to my mother?" Luke had asked Emma the next day.

Emma had reminded him they were both in a dangerous, unpredictable situation with a clearly unhinged man. Running was the only option.

Still, Luke carried around the weight of his decision. He also seemed to go back and forth about telling the police, or at least his father. But every time he circled back to what the man said, he decided to keep what happened between the two of them.

Emma had been trying her best to keep Luke from worrying too much, but with his mother's life potentially on the line, how much could she really say or do?

Luke had asked her earlier that day if she would be at the barn in the evening, and if so, if he could watch her ride Lexington. Emma had promised to be there right after school and they could spend some time together after her ride.

Emma walked across the grass towards the barn. She could already see Lexington's dropped lip and sleepy expression as she walked in.

"Hey bud," Emma murmured, running her hand up his forelock. His ears swiveled in her direction and he nuzzled her pockets for treats.

"Emma."

The tone of Luke's voice made her turn around quickly. "Luke? What is it?"

Luke looked pale, like someone had punched him in the stomach. Something had most definitely happened, and it clearly wasn't good.

He pulled a piece of white, lined paper from his pocket and handed it to her. Emma felt her stomach drop, knowing already who it was from.

Her eyes ran over the words, feeling more nauseous with each word she read.

Luke,

Don't you know it's rude to leave before a conversation is over? Your mother should have taught you better.

If you want to see her alive, meet me at the address on the back of this note tomorrow at 5:00 pm sharp.

And this time, I'll be sure to bring her.

If you run this time, you'll never see her again.

He didn't try to mask his handwriting this time. Emma looked up at Luke, eyes wide.

"Did you get this today?" Emma asked.

"I found it right before you got here. It was wedged in my screen door."

Emma remembered the conversation she had with Luke the day after the run in with this mystery man. The lack of postage on the original letter delivered to the school had led them to an eerie conclusion – he more than likely knew where Luke lived. Emma was sure Luke hadn't slept at all knowing that, and that it probably made it that much harder to not tell his dad. But Luke had said he was sure that if he told his dad, that his dad would call the police. If anything happened to his mom because of it, Luke said he would never forgive himself.

So for the time being, he had decided to play by this creep's rules.

"Do you really think he has your mom?" Emma asked. It was something she had wondered since that day. Could this whole thing be a con?

"I don't know. What I do know is that he knows too much about her. Plus, the timing of her sending that letter to me and him showing up out of the blue not long after makes me think it's possible. I just don't think I could risk her life with the information pointing towards him telling the truth, you know?" Luke replied.

Emma rested a hand on Luke's shoulder. "What if this is a trap, Luke?"

Luke shook his head. "I know that's possible. But if he really has my mom...," Luke's voice broke with emotion.

"I get it. Well, you aren't going alone, that's for sure," Emma replied.

Luke's eyes widened. "No way I am putting you in danger again."

"Too bad. We're in this together, remember? Which means we need to come up with a plan just in case things go wrong. Do we know where this place is?"

Luke flipped over the paper and studied the address again. "Actually, I know exactly where this is. My mom used to take me trail riding here as a kid. It's called Lobdell Reserve."

"See? Looks like we will be going in on horseback, which is a huge advantage. Plus, Maggie has taken us there a few times. Good thing your girlfriend rides horses too, right?" Emma teased, trying to lighten the mood.

"I still don't like the idea of getting you involved in all this, Emma."

"You aren't getting me involved. I already involved myself, remember?"

Luke tossed her a look. "I guess so," he mumbled.

Emma noticed just how dark the circles under his eyes were becoming. Poor Luke. If he went out there alone in this chaos, there was no way he was going to be able to get his mom back safely. If she was actually out there, that is.

"Let's come up with a plan, and then you need to go to bed," Emma said.

"Is it that obvious? I feel like I haven't slept in days," Luke replied.

"That's because you probably haven't. Come on, let's figure out the plan so you can get some rest."

Emma and Luke spent the next thirty minutes talking about every scenario they could think of, and what they could do in each of them. Since there would be no cell service out on the trails, surely what the man had planned purposely, there would be no way to call for help if things went south.

"With these escape plans, I think we can take this guy. I mean, he seems kind of reckless, right? If he slips up, we'll have him," Emma reassured Luke who looked like he could fall asleep standing up at this point.

"I hope so," Luke replied.

Emma stood up and offered Luke her hand to help him up. For once, he was the weaker of the two of them.

"Go get some rest now, ok? We need you on your game tomorrow, Luke Cromwell."

"Thanks Emma. I hope you know how much this means to me...how much *you* mean to me."

Emma reached her hand up and gently touched Luke's cheek. "I've never felt about anyone else the way I feel about you. I'll run headlong into danger with you any day."

Emma pressed her lips to Luke's, giving him a featherlight kiss. Luke wrapped his arms around her waist, pulling her to his chest.

"I'll see you tomorrow," he said with a weak smile.

Emma watched as he walked slowly toward his house.

Tomorrow was the day that hopefully Luke could finally get his mother back after all these years. That is, if the creepy guy holding her hostage didn't outsmart them first.

"That's not going to happen," she thought, trying to convince herself.

"I think that's everything," Emma said, shutting the trailer door.

The squeaking and then banging sound of the trailer's rear doors being closed and locked could be heard behind her.

"I'm good back here too," Luke replied.

A wave of nerves washed over her. What they were about to do was very danger-ous, she knew that yesterday when she had agreed to come. But suddenly, it felt *real*.

"No backing out now," she thought.

"Ready?" Luke asked, opening the truck door for her.

"Ready," she said, feeling less confident than she sounded as she climbed into the passenger seat.

"The trail head is only ten minutes from here," Luke said before he shut the truck door.

A shiver ran up her spine. "That's good," she replied, her mouth suddenly feeling dry. What was she about to face?

"What did you tell your dad about taking the truck and trailer?" Emma asked, hoping the question would distract her from her other thoughts.

"I said you wanted me to haul you to go trail riding and that you didn't want to ride alone. He knows we're dating now, so he didn't say too much about it, surprisingly. I think he actually likes you, which is saying something," Luke said, his goofy grin making an appearance for the first time in days.

Emma smiled back. "Good. I was wondering how we were going to pull that off."

The truck and trailer's tires crunched against the gravel driveway as they pulled away from the barn.

The ten minutes it took to get to the Lobdell Reserve trail head seemed to fly by. Before Emma knew it, they were unloading the horses and tacking them up.

Emma swung her leg over Lexington and Luke mounted up on his horse, Ducky, as well. They headed out onto the main trail, both scanning the area for any signs or sounds from the man or Luke's mom. This part of the trail was mainly open fields with tall grass.

"I wonder how deep into the trail he is," Emma whispered. How were they supposed to find them when the trail forked?

"I would guess far enough in that no one can hear her yelling," Luke said. The tension in the air seemed to thicken after he spoke.

What *had* she gotten herself into? Still, could she really have sat at home and let Luke come out here all alone? No way.

"Luke, look!" Emma said, holding her reins in one had as she pointed. The first fork in the trail was ahead, and a single orange cone sat on the far right side of one of the paths.

"I guess that's our clue?" Luke said, steering Ducky towards the marked path.

"Seems like it," Emma whispered back.

They headed silently down the marked path. Pine trees lined either side of the now heavily-wooded part of the trail.

An eerie feeling began creeping in the deeper into the forest they went. Now that the scenery had changed to the type conducive for holding someone hostage, it seemed like they could stumble onto them at any moment.

Luke's voice breaking the silence unexpectedly made her jump. "There's another cone over there."

Emma's gaze followed Luke's to a cone that was set to the far left of the path. It marked what looked like one of those narrow, off-the-beaten-path-trails or maybe even a deer trail.

"Do you think that's from him?" Emma asked, eyeing the sketchy looking trail.

"I guess there's really only one way to find out," Luke replied.

Emma took a deep breath as she followed behind Luke as he steered Ducky towards the new trail. Neither spoke as they listened to every crack of a branch or rustling in the leaves. The path led into an even deeper part of the forest, and the path seemed to barely be big enough for the horses to make their way through without branches brushing against their riders.

Emma felt her palms begin to feel clammy as they rode on. Being in such a confined part of the trail and knowing the man could be anywhere felt beyond unnerving.

Finally, Emma could see a break in the thick forest ahead. As they got closer, she could see a clearing and a small field surrounded by more thick forest.

Emma hear Luke catch his breath. "Mom," he breathed.

The blood drained from Emma's face as she tried to peer around Luke and Ducky in front of her to get a better look. Just ahead of where the trees gave way to the clearing, a woman sat cross-legged on the ground with her hands tied behind her back. Still trying to see, Emma shifted her weight in the saddle, standing in her stirrups to see if she could find the man who had to be nearby.

"Where is he? Do you see him?" Emma whispered to Luke.

"No, I don't see him anywhere" Luke whispered back.

Ducky and Luke walked into the open area with Emma and Lexington on their heels. Emma scanned the clearing, looking for the man and suddenly feeling very vulnerable. Where was he? Certainly he hadn't left Luke's mom half-tied and alone.

"Luke, get out of here! This is what he wants!" Luke's mother hissed, her own gaze sweeping the clearing.

"Mom," Luke croaked, sliding off his horse. His eyes were wide as he ran to his mother.

"Luke, you should get back on Ducky," Emma called nervously. What was he thinking? But that seemed to be precisely the problem; he wasn't thinking. Luke dropped was dropping to his knees now in front of his mother, tears welling in his eyes.

"Luke, you need to leave," his mother begged again, tears in her own eyes now.

"I'm not leaving you!" Luke said, going behind his mother now as he tried to tug at the rope that bound her hands.

That was the moment Emma knew she was on her own. Luke was blinded by seeing his mother and trying to set her free. But Emma and Luke's mother could see what Luke couldn't, despite their warnings.

Luke pulled the pocket knife from his pocket, using it in a sawing motion in an attempt to cut the rope.

"Isn't this a lovely reunion," a man's voice said. A rustling sound followed as he emerged from some tall brush nearby.

Emma flinched but didn't feel startled. Of course he had been hiding, waiting for Luke to do exactly what he was doing right now.

"Luke!" Emma begged, but Luke didn't hear her. He was still frantically trying to cut the ropes on his mother's wrists.

"I'm sorry you had to be caught up in this, but one way or another you will need to leave. This is a family matter," the man said to Emma, before he continued toward Luke and his mom.

Emma was suddenly having regrets about not calling the police. Why had she been so stupid? They had walked right into his trap! But Luke had insisted, begging her not to for fear his mother's life would be put in jeopardy.

"Luke, please," Emma croaked out. The man was almost to Luke and his mother now.

"My, we have a lot to talk about, don't we Lainie?" the man said, looking directly at Luke's mother.

Luke's mother's eyes narrowed. "Stay away from my son. You can take me, but please, leave him!"

"Now, what kind of family reunion would that be?" the man said.

Family reunion? Was this guy on drugs? Or delusional? Did he really think Luke and his mother were his family?

"Who are you?" Emma blurted out. Her hand flew over her mouth. Had she just said that out loud?

The man smirked but barely looked up from Luke and his mother, whom he now towered over.

"In time, girl," he said with a chuckle.

Luke stood up holding the pocket knife out in front of him. "Stay away from her!"

The man backhanded Luke across the face, almost knocking him off his feet and launching his pocket knife into the grass. Luke stumbled backwards, trying to regain balance, but dropped to his knees.

"Lainie, I think it's time you enlighten this boy on a few things if you want him to keep his teeth," the man sneered, picking up the pocket knife. Luke's mother began crying.

Emma twitched, almost sending Lexington forward toward Luke. But in order to stick to their plan, the man couldn't be quite so close to Luke and his mother. That is, if Luke remembered it too.

"Please, don't...," Luke's mother begged in between sobs.

The man's face went from slightly amused to beat red. "You answer my questions, or you leave your son without a mother. Your choice." Luke's mother nodded, then lowered her head.

Luke wiped away the blood tricking from his nose as he slowly stood up again.

"First question," the man said, resting his weight on one foot. He paused, seeming to consider what he wanted to ask first. "Were we lovers once?" he said with a grin.

Luke's mother nodded. Luke's eyes widened as he looked over at his mother.

"I want to hear you say it!" the man screamed, inches from her face.

"Yes," she croaked.

"Good," the man said, seemingly pleased.

"What?" Luke breathed.

Luke's mother opened her mouth to respond but was cut off.

"Question two. Who put me in prison?"

Luke's mother hesitated. "I did."

"And why?"

"You drugged a horse! You almost killed...," Luke's mother began.

"That's enough! I did what I had to do to win, to make the money we needed...,"
The man caught himself and paused.

"Next question." This time, the man's smile broadened, an almost giddy look was
on his face. "What is the biggest lie you've ever told?"

Sobs shook Luke's mother. "Answer!" he screamed, raising his hand as he took a
step towards Luke again.

Lainie turned towards Luke. "I'm so sorry, Luke. I never wanted this to be how you
found out."

"Mom?"

"I lied to you Luke. This man's name is Joe...and he is your biological father."

Luke's jaw dropped. "No, he can't be...,"

"I know this is a lot to process, but it's true. We met at the track. He was a groom,
and I was buying one of the Thoroughbreds that the trainer he worked for was
retiring. Luke, I didn't know he was ever capable of hurting a horse then or that
he could be such a monster...,"

Joe took one more step towards Luke's mother. "Enough! Stop making me the bad guy here! *You* turned in the father of your unborn child! The only monster here is *you*!"

Joe turned on his heels and grabbed Luke's arm. "You and your mother are coming with me. It's time the family reunited, don't you think?" A sickly smile tugged at the man's lips.

Joe shoved Luke onto the ground before he walked back towards the brush he had originally come from. Seconds later, a horse, who had presumably been tied to a nearby tree, was led behind him.

"I'm not going with you!" Luke stood up as he yelled, spitting in Joe's face when he was close enough. Joe punched Luke in the stomach and Luke dropped to his knees.

Emma gasped. *"Now Luke!"* she thought.

Was he so wrapped up in the emotions of what was happening? Would he remember their plan? The man didn't see her as a threat, and why would he? A seventeen year old girl seemingly unarmed? But this was precisely what they had hoped for. The backup plan needed to happen now, or it wasn't happening at all.

Joe pulled a rope from the saddle bag attached to the horse. It was obvious that this was it. He planned to take Luke and his mother with him to God knows where. Had this been his plan all along? To trick Luke into coming out here so he could kidnap them both?

Emma held her breath and bit her lip to keep herself from yelling at Luke to do what he needed to. They were running out of time.

Luke clutched his stomach and looked up at Joe with a fiery expression. "No," he breathed.

In the blink of an eye Emma saw Luke push himself off the ground and rotate his body slightly before roundhouse kicking Joe behind his knee. Joe lost his balance, eyes wide as he hunched over. Luke balanced back, then kneed him in the groin.

Joe dropped to his knees.

This was it. Emma sent Lexington forward at full speed.

"Now!" she thought, swinging her leg over the saddle for an emergency dismount, landing on her feet. She was suddenly grateful for all the times Maggie had made them practice that.

Emma pulled out the pocket-sized taser her father had given her the day she started driving her car alone for the first time. Taking two steps forward, she closed the gap and pushed the taser into the man's side. Joe groaned and dropped the rest of the way to the ground, his body recoiling from the electric shock.

"Lexington!" Emma called, turning around. She breathed a sigh of relief when she saw her horse had stopped not far from where she had jumped off, still looking surprised by his owner's sudden dismount. Emma remembered her father saying the taser's affect might last a few seconds to a few minutes, which meant they needed to get out of there. Now.

Luke had already helped his mother up and was running towards his horse. Using his interlocked palms, Luke gave his mother a boost into the saddle as she used her knee to push off his hands. Luke used the stirrup to swing his leg up and over to sit behind the saddle, gathering his reins on either side of his mother.

Emma turned toward her horse again, taking one step toward Lexington.

"Emma!" Luke's voice called out to her across the clearing.

She suddenly felt a hand wrap around her ankle a split second before falling face first toward the ground. Her heart hammered in her chest as she turned her head to see Joe still on the ground, but his hand was wrapped around her leg.

Recoiling her leg back, Emma kicked out as hard as she could, the heel of her riding boot making contact with the hand he had wrapped around her. Joe groaned again and pulled his hand away.

Clawing the ground, Emma scrambled up and beelined toward her horse at full speed. Shoving her foot in the stirrup, she pushed off of it with all her strength, barely pulling herself up into the saddle of the tall horse.

Emma and Luke made eye contact, and then Luke wrapped his legs around Ducky, sending him towards the path they came from. Emma took one last look at the man on the ground who was already starting to recover as he pushed himself up off the ground.

Emma made a kissing sound to Lexington as she sent him forward and away from the man who would no doubt be on their tails on his own horse within seconds. Horse hooves pounding against the dry dirt below them was all she could hear now.

Blue and red lights bounced off the side of the barn.

"We have him in custody, and they found the horse too," Emma heard a police officer say to Luke's father.

Luke held an ice pack up to his face, removing it only to answer the questions the police officer in front of him was asking.

"Thank you for your time," the police officer said, glancing first at Luke, then Emma. Emma took Luke's hand and squeezed it as they exchanged a look of relief.

Across the driveway, Emma saw Luke's mother was also being released from questioning. Mr. Crowell was now standing a few feet away, waiting for his long-lost wife to be finished. Lainie stood up and wrapped her arms around Luke's father's neck. Emma smiled to herself as she watched their reunion.

Hand in hand, Luke's parents walked towards where she and Luke were seated on a bench against the barn.

"I suppose I have a lot of explaining to do," Luke's mother said with a sad smile. She glanced at Emma, then back to Luke.

"It's ok mom, whatever you need to say you can say in front of Emma."

Lainie nodded, then sat on the bench next to Luke, resting a hand softly on his shoulder.

"Everything Joe said is true. He is, in fact, your biological father," she said, a crease forming between her eyes.

Luke glanced at his father and then at his mother again. "Your father knows you are not biologically his. He's always known," Lainie smiled up at her husband.

"I don't understand," Luke said, frowning.

Lainie smiled weakly. "When I met Joe, I didn't know what he was capable of. I was young, and maybe a little naïve, and he was charming. But then I caught him drugging a horse so he would have the upper hand in a race one day. Back then, drugging horses on the track was much more common and harder to test. I told him if he didn't tell the trainer what he had done, and scratch the horse from the race, then I would. But the horse ended up at the starting gate anyway, and when I stepped in, that's when things took a turn for the worse. A fight broke out on the track, your father was involved in it actually, and Joe was arrested. Joe had beaten someone to the point that we wondered if that man would make it. It was the trainer your father worked for at the time and a dear friend to him. I had found out only weeks earlier that I was pregnant. When I told your father, he and I had been getting closer and just started dating. We decided to get married and keep your biological father a secret, for your sake."

Luke's stunned expression bounced from his father back to his mother. "So why did you leave us then?"

"Joe got out of prison finally and when I found out, I knew he would come looking for me. I decided there was no other way to keep you and your father safe than to vanish. I know it sounds extreme, but I knew Joe well enough to know he would never stop looking until he found me and got his revenge."

"So how did he find you after all these years?" Emma asked.

Lainie shook her head. "That was my fault. I sent Luke that letter during a moment of weakness. I didn't put my return address, hoping that would be enough, but the city and state were still listed on the postage. Eventually, he did find me because of it. But what I didn't know is that he had found Luke first a while ago and had been watching him, I'm guessing waiting for me to reach out. I'm so sorry Luke, I left you defenseless and I thought I was doing what was best for you at the time. For both of you...," Lainie's voice broke mid-sentence as she looked at both Luke and her husband.

Emma watched the hard expression that seemed permanent on Luke's father's face soften for the first time since she'd met him years ago. He dropped to his knees and wrapped both his hands around Lainie's. "You're home now. That's all that matters."

Mr. Cromwell turned to Luke. "I owe you an apology, Luke. When you mother left...well, it broke something inside of me. I wasn't the father you needed me to be, and I took it out on you far too often. You just look so much like your mother..," Luke's father trailed off, shaking his head.

Luke stood up and embraced his father. "I forgive you, dad," he said.

Emma smiled as the two held each other close for what she assumed was the first time in a very long time.

Emma's legs swung back and forth on the boat dock she sat on as she stared at the water-colored painted looking sunset above them. It had already been the perfect first day of summer, spent out on Luke's father's boat with him and his family.

"You're right, this might be the best view of the sunset I've ever seen," she whispered.

"I told you it was," Luke whispered back, wrapping an arm around her shoulders. The lake in front of them reflected the pink and orange of the sky above it.

Emma looked over at Luke. "It's strange to think that a few weeks ago we were preparing to find your mom and face up to that Joe guy."

Luke shook his head. "I know, it's been such a surreal few weeks having my mom home again. You should see my parents, dancing around the kitchen and acting like teenagers again. It's a little nauseating," he said with a smirk.

"It sounds like they are happy," Emma replied, smiling.

"I think they are. So am I, though," Luke said, pulling Emma a little closer.

"Me too," she replied.

Emma rested her head on Luke's shoulder as the last of the light began fading from the sky.

"I couldn't have saved her without you. I'm not sure I ever said this out loud, but thank you Emma."

Emma lifted her head to meet Luke's gaze. She studied his expression and thought about that day and how she'd felt. After having weeks of normalcy after that fateful day, Emma felt ready to say something she had been feeling for a little while now.

"I love you Luke Cromwell. Of course I was going to follow you right into danger."

Luke's eyes widened and a huge grin spread across his face. "I love you too, Emma Walker."

He leaned closer, hooking his finger under her chin. Her eyes met his, holding his gaze a moment before his lips pressed firmly against hers, moving slowly.

They say when you're young, you view the world differently. Your emotions, your perspective, your entire life is one way, and then when you become a real adult, all of that changes.

Emma wasn't sure if Luke was what people refer to as "the one," but even if he wasn't and they went their separate ways one day, Emma knew she would never be the same. She had a taste of what love was like. She had felt how it took over her mind and heart in a way she never could have imagined.

Luke pulled away and looked her in the eyes, his warm, genuine smile making her heart flutter.

Emma was glad that, if nothing else, Luke was the person she would look back on years later as the boy who taught her what love was.

The End

"The Impelled Series" continues in book one of the series, titled "Impelled."

If you have already read the first three books in the series, be on the lookout for upcoming new books written from the point of view of other characters from the series telling their stories.

Be sure to subscribe to my newsletter on my website, sarahwelkbaynumauthor.com, and follow my author page on Amazon for updates on new releases!

Notes from the Author

Thank you to the readers who took a chance and read my debut series. I hope you enjoyed reading it as much as I loved writing it!

If you enjoyed it, please be sure to leave a review so others have a chance to find it as well. Reviews help me tremendously as an independently published author and it also helps other readers.

I look forward to bringing you lots of new and exciting books in this and other series in the future!

Sincerely,

Sarah Welk Baynum

Subscribe to my newsletter (sign up form on my website home page) to be the first to know about the release date for the next book in this, and other series!

https://sarahwelkbaynumauthor.com/

About the Author

Sarah Welk Baynum has an extensive equestrian background which became the inspiration behind her debut novel "Impelled."

While writing her novels, Sarah draws from previous experience as a working student, show groom, barn manager, working for FarmVet and other various jobs in the horse industry over the years both in her hometown and in Wellington & Ocala, Florida. Sarah also attended Otterbein University and majored in Equine Business and Facility Management.

Sarah still owns horses and actively competes in show jumping and three-day eventing, and horses have been a big part of her life since the age of twelve. Her first horse may have been a gelding, but she has a bias for mares and has primarily owned mares throughout the years.

Besides writing equestrian novels, Sarah also writes articles for numerous equestrian magezines.

When she isn't writing or riding, Sarah also enjoys competing in local and national singing competitions, and mainly sings country music.

Today, Sarah lives in her hometown just outside of Columbus, Ohio, with her family which includes her husband, her two dogs, two cats and her two mares Tilly (a warmblood) and Letty (an off the track thoroughbred).

Printed in Great Britain
by Amazon

19721422R00120